BAD APPLE

BY

BOOK 4 IN THE UNCERTAIN SAINTS SERIES

LANI LYNN VALE

ISBN-13: 978-1537157696

ISBN-10: 1537157698

Dedication

This has to be the hardest part of writing this book. I struggle every time when I get to this page in my word document. Who the hell do you thank for giving you everything you ever dreamed of?

My readers: Hell yes, this wouldn't be possible without y'all.

My mom: Thank you for being there for me. Thank you for letting me move back in after you thought you got rid of me.

My mother in law: Yeah, y'all can thank the shit out of her. I likely wouldn't be writing right now if she hadn't gotten me hooked on reading.

My husband: You may drive me nuts, but I love you anyways. There are no limits to my love. Even when you piss me off. It's always there. I hope you know that.

Acknowledgements

Furiousfotog: This photo is gorgeous. Thank you so much for sharing your talent with the world.

Alex Minsky: The same goes for you. You really made this character come to life. Thank you for sharing yourself with us, too.

Danielle P.: You seriously have no clue what you mean to me. Thank you so much for everything you do.

CONTENTS

Chapter 1- Page 9
Chapter 2- Page 27
Chapter 3- Page 43
Chapter 4- Page 49
Chapter 5- Page 61
Chapter 6- Page 79
Chapter 7- Page 105
Chapter 8- Page 115
Chapter 9- Page 121
Chapter 10- Page 133
Chapter 11- Page 147
Chapter 12- Page 159
Chapter 13- Page 167
Chapter 14- Page 201
Chapter 15- Page 215
Chapter 16- Page 219
Chapter 17- Page 233
Chapter 18- Page 241
Chapter 19- Page 257
Chapter 20- Page 265
Chapter 21- Page 281
Chapter 22- Page 293
Chapter 23- Page 301
Epilogue- Page 319

Other titles by Lani Lynn Vale:
The Freebirds

Boomtown

Highway Don't Care

Another One Bites the Dust

Last Day of My Life

Texas Tornado

I Don't Dance

The Heroes of The Dixie Wardens MC

Lights To My Siren

Halligan To My Axe

Kevlar To My Vest

Keys To My Cuffs

Life To My Flight

Charge To My Line

Counter To My Intelligence

Right To My Wrong

Code 11- KPD SWAT

Center Mass

Double Tap

Bang Switch

Execution Style

Charlie Foxtrot

Kill Shot

Coup De Grace

The Uncertain Saints

Whiskey Neat

Jack & Coke

Vodka On The Rocks

Bad Apple

Dirty Mother

Rusty Nail

The Kilgore Fire Series

Shock Advised

Flash Point

Oxygen Deprived

Controlled Burn

Put Out

I Like Big Dragons Series

I Like Big Dragons and I Cannot Lie

Dragons Need Love, Too

Oh, My Dragon

CHAPTER 1

Everyone's brave until they figure out the roach has wings.
-Fact of Life

Kitt

I walked into The Uncertain Saints' club house, completely expecting that I would get trashed.

What I didn't expect, though, was to get pregnant.

However, life works in mysterious ways.

Ways that seem to take a hold of you and shake you until you get your shit straight.

That was what Apple Drew, aka Core, was to me…the shake up I needed to get my head on straight.

I was going to school to become a family law paralegal and I was on the verge of quitting.

When I'd started going to school to become a paralegal, they never told me that I'd have to deal with the kind of trash that I did on a daily basis.

Today, for instance, I realized that maybe family law just wasn't for me.

People were assholes, pure and simple.

And all I wanted to do was see my brother.

My brother who'd bet me that I wouldn't come.

But I'd show him how wrong he was.

I smiled at the man that opened the door for me.

"Hey, Mig!" I waved excitedly. "How's the baby?"

Mig smiled, and his wife, Annie, came up behind him and wrapped her arms around his waist.

"The baby is being a rotten turd," Annie offered as she stuck her head under Mig's arm. "He takes after his father."

Mig snorted.

"That's what you say every time he keeps you up all night," Mig said to his wife. "But then he starts walking two months before most kids, and you say he takes after you."

Annie grinned unrepentantly. "Yeah," she admitted. "I do do that, don't I?"

I skittered past them into the main room of the clubhouse.

The place itself was located just off of Caddo River, a nifty little river/lake that ran from Texas all the way down to the Gulf of Mexico.

A long time ago, the river was used to transport goods that were sold in the southern states. It was a main source of income for the small town of Uncertain, Texas.

However, over time, it had become just another river until a few years ago, when bad things started happening in all the cities that the Caddo ran through.

It was suspected that the river was a main transport route for illegal goods.

Since the river was relatively unsupervised, a lot of the time people got away with their illegal activities.

Then The Uncertain Saints got involved, effectively tearing a hole in the bad guys' plans.

The clubhouse was deliberately located on the river in a very popular part which saw a lot of traffic.

The building stood on stilts that lifted the entire thing up one story. It resembled more of a beach house, which was unexpected on a lake, but I loved it.

It wasn't old, per se, but it had quite a bit of that old feel to it.

When the Saints had built it, they'd used reclaimed wood from old houses and barns in the construction.

Now, although it was less than ten years old, it looked more like it was hundreds.

"Hey sweetheart," my brother, Ridley, called.

I turned to find him staring at me with an expectant look on his face.

I sighed and pulled a Hershey's bar out of my pocket and handed it to him.

"Happy?" I asked.

He glared at me.

"I don't mind you living in my house..." I interrupted him before he could get any more words that might offend me out of that stupid mouth of his.

"It's our house," I snapped. "It's no more your house than my house."

He shrugged.

"Papaw signed it over to me, and you know it," he shrugged, knowing it would rile me up.

I ignored him and walked to the cooler that was sitting out on the back deck that overlooked the river.

Lifting the lid, I reached in and grabbed a Mike's Hard Lemonade that my brother most likely bought specifically for me.

The ladies who had recently started becoming permanent fixtures in The Uncertain Saints MC were more wine drinkers.

I was most likely the only one that drank actual 'wiener drinks', as my brother liked to call my beverage of choice.

Apparently, there wasn't as much alcohol in it, and he liked to tell me that all the time.

He also didn't like that I always had my drinks on hand at home, but we never seemed to have any of his.

Yes, my brother and I lived together.

No, neither of us had anyone.

And yes, I have brought men home. Well, only two.

My brother didn't bring any women home, but it had more to do with the fact that he was still in love with his dead wife.

I'd just closed the cooler lid when I heard the new prospect.

Well, I didn't know for sure if it was him, but the plain leather vest on the man's back was a good indication he was the one my brother had been telling me about.

He'd been there for a while, but this was my first club party in well over six months.

He was clearly comfortable here, and by the look of all the ladies crawling all over him, he was popular to boot.

Then he had to go and open that mouth of his, and at the sound of his deep, raspy voice raced down my spine causing me to shiver.

I immediately took my drink and headed the other way, not wanting to get caught up in the mess that usually was a prospect.

The Uncertain Saints didn't let many people into their fold.

In fact, there were only six members total in the club, and none of them seemed to have the time or inclination to add more to their group.

I knew there had to be some kind of special circumstances for the men of the Uncertain Saints to even consider adding that man to the group.

Which meant he was fucked up.

And I didn't do fucked up.

I had my own fucked up to deal with.

Kind of like quitting my job.

Two hours and four hard lemonades later, I was feeling quite nice.

I hadn't thought about my job once, and I was having a great time watching the comings and goings.

"Why the long face?" The man I'd been studiously avoiding all night, Apple, asked.

I turned my face and shrugged. "Nothing."

And at that point, there really was nothing wrong.

"You look like you're about to kill someone," the annoying man observed.

I shrugged, picking at the invisible lint on my shoulder before I picked up my spoon and shoveled another bite of the chicken spaghetti someone had made into my mouth.

It was pretty good, but it wasn't like Papaw fixed it.

There was good, and then there was *good.* And this wasn't it.

We sat next to each other in companionable silence as we both ate our food.

I glanced over at the man's plate and nearly laughed when I saw how much food was on it.

His helping of food mounded high on his plate, and I feared for the integrity of the Styrofoam that was straining to maintain its form under the weight of all that food.

"What are you looking at?" He grumbled, not bothering to turn his face.

Instead he kept shoveling his food into his mouth in a great imitation of a Hoover Vacuum

"I was just wondering if you left any for the rest of them," I waved my hand at the room absently, going back to my food.

"Everyone has already eaten," he muttered. "Apparently, when you're a prospect, you eat last."

"Hmm," I drawled. "Imagine that."

He snorted.

"Why are you a prospect, anyway?" I asked.

"Because I want to be," he muttered, and I felt the instant coolness that came with the words.

I didn't say anything else, only went back to eating my food.

It was him that went back to the companionable silence, the weird wall of tension between us slowly dissipating until the only thing left was awareness.

He was a sexy man.

He was tall with unusual blonde hair that I couldn't decide whether or not had a hint of red running through it.

He had a blonde beard that was trimmed close to his face, and wasn't over the top like some of the others in the MC.

He had light blue eyes that were rimmed with a hint of green and a very muscular body.

Not Hulk muscular, but a nicely toned body that looked to be from working rather than working out.

Not that I didn't think he did one over the other. He just didn't look like he was the type of guy to go to the gym all the time.

"So what do you do?" I asked curiously.

"I'm a game warden…and a lumberjack," he muttered, slurping up another forkful of chicken spaghetti.

"A lumberjack?" I asked. "Is that even a real occupation anymore?"

He turned to look at me.

"Yes."

One word was all I received, and I knew better than to continue on that line of questioning.

"I'm in school to become a paralegal," I told him, sensing a change of subject was needed.

"Yeah," he murmured. "I heard."

"You did?" I asked in confusion. *Had I already told him that?*

No.

He nodded. "Your brother, Ridley, told me."

I blinked.

Ridley didn't often talk about me to other people.

I was a very private person, but then again, having what I had, and experiencing what I did, there was a good reason for it.

"Oh," was the only thing I could think to say.

"He said you hate doing it," he commented.

I snorted.

"Yeah, you could say that."

"Then why do you do it?"

He was a persistent bastard.

"Because I need the job…and the money," I said, raising my brows at him.

And it was hard to find a job that would work around my ailment.

"What's so bad about it?" He pushed his plate away from him.

It was completely empty and looked almost as if he'd licked the damn thing.

"You really wanna know?" I wondered.

He nodded.

"Well, my day started off a little like this: I walked into the building to hear a man say, 'You're always looking for a man to sweep you off your feet. Well, let me tell you something, woman!'" I imitated the way the man had sounded. "'Sweeping is your job!'"

And that had been the turning point…the fork in the road, as one would say.

"I knew, as soon as I heard the man say that, that it wasn't going to be a good case. Then he'd gone and proved me right by continuing to verbally beat down his wife over and over again, forcing her to agree to his edicts, all because he controlled the money and she didn't," I sighed, dropping my head into my hands. "I hate it. But I like it all at the same time. I like helping my clients win. I like my part in helping the kids get what they deserve."

Apple nodded.

"I'm not a full time lumberjack," he said finally, going back to our earlier topic. "But my dad's business is his livelihood, and if I'm not there to do it, he can't pay his bills."

That made more sense, and I now had a reason for him and his reluctance to speak more on the subject.

He got up and grabbed himself a beer from the cooler, along with another drink for me.

He handed them both to me as a commotion at the front of the room had me smiling as another member's wife, Tasha, was giving her husband, Casten, the verbal smack down.

She was a fireball, that was for sure.

"Thank you," I muttered, reaching for the bottle to twist the lid off.

He took it back out of my hands and twisted the top of effortlessly before handing it back without another word.

I thanked him again before taking another sip.

I was going to regret drinking in the morning, without a doubt. But I couldn't get my thoughts sorted out, and to do that, I needed to let go a little bit.

"Are they fighting about goats?" He asked.

I nodded. "She wants some, and he doesn't."

"I can tell that," he sipped his beer. "But don't they live in the city."

I nodded. "She saw a video last week about a goat as a house pet. The owners even took them on walks and everything."

"Interesting," he murmured. "I have goats."

"You do?" I asked.

He nodded. "Yeah, but they're not pets."

I smiled, unable to help myself.

Hearing that this big badass in his tight red t-shirt, faded blue jeans that had holes in both the knees, as well as where I guessed his keys were held in his pockets, with his tight leather vest had goats really made me want to laugh.

He was the exact opposite of what I expected him to be when I walked into the clubhouse today.

Fun, came to mind.

I drank my lemonade, smiling from time to time when the man would have something funny to say.

And when he asked me to help him start picking up the trash, I didn't even hesitate. I just helped him.

My brother gave me a weird look, but ultimately ignored me for the conversation he was having with a few men from the police department.

People started to leave, and the only ones left, by the time I thought it sufficiently clean enough, were my brother, Peek, the president, and his wife, Casten and his wife, Mig and his wife, Apple and me.

"Thanks for the help," Apple thanked me genuinely.

I shrugged and picked up a new bottle of lemonade from the cooler, then sat on the only open seat, which happened to be the fireplace ledge.

Apple started to lean against the mantle, but I moved over slightly giving him room to sit next to me.

Although it was a tight fit, he didn't complain.

"Thanks," he grunted.

I nodded, too busy smelling him to say 'you're welcome.'

"I think we should go on a fun run two weeks from now," Peek boomed, bringing everyone's attention to him. "We haven't gone on one in a couple of months, and now that everyone's finally free of babies and shit, I want to go. To Arizona."

"What's in Arizona?" I found myself asking.

It's not like I was invited to go.

In fact, I hadn't ever been on the back of a motorcycle.

My brother was too scared of the possible consequences of me falling off during one of my 'fits', as he liked to call them, that I never bothered asking him anymore.

I peeled the label off my bottle, completely forgetting that I'd even asked a question until the room got silent around me, finally making me pull my head up in confusion.

They were all staring at me.

Even the newbie.

"What?" I mumbled.

My brother was the one to answer.

"Mr. Prospect here just asked you if you wanted to ride with him to Arizona," Ridley teased, making it sound like he knew I would turn him down. "And to answer your question, nothing's in Arizona. We just like to go to different places and see the sights."

My brother's face looked so superior, so sure of himself, that I wanted to knock him down a notch.

He was always doing that, acting like he knew what was best for me, and it was suffocating.

So I put my foot into it.

"I'd love to," I turned my head to see Apple staring at me expectantly.

His eyes showed surprise, and then satisfaction…and then worry.

He looked over at my brother, then back to me.

"Am I missing something?" He asked.

I grinned.

"No," I smiled. "Not anything important."

"You're not like a psycho or anything, right?" He asked for confirmation.

I shook my head.

"Not the last time I checked," I baited.

"You've checked to see if you're psycho?" He tilted his head slightly.

I shrugged.

"I've taken a few of those quizzes on Facebook that make you pick a bunch of pictures and answer random questions. According to them, I am not a psycho," I returned.

Chuckles rose around the room as Apple and I sparred back and forth, but then I made a faux pas of sorts.

I asked about his name.

"So, tell me about your name," I broke in. "Is it a family name?"

I hadn't meant it as anything but what it was. A fucking question.

Did Apple take it like that? *No.*

He took immediate offense to the fact that I would question where he got his name, automatically assuming that I was being rude.

"My name came from my mother, thank you very much," he muttered, standing up. "If y'all don't need anything else, my Pop's all by himself tonight."

Peek automatically nodded, and I was left wondering what in the hell just happened.

"Ummm," I floundered. "Do y'all think I'm still invited this weekend?"

Annie, Mig's wife, giggled.

"No," she snickered. "I don't think you will be."

I snapped my fingers.

"Damn," I moaned. "The first time I get an invitation by someone that has all his teeth and it's rescinded within the hour."

Laughter followed that comment, but I wasn't feeling very 'laughy' at the moment.

I was actually hurt.

I always went out of my way to be nice to people and to have someone think I was purposefully being mean didn't sit well with me.

But when I got up to follow Apple outside, he was gone, and all that was left was the smell of burnt rubber and a wallet.

***

"Thanks," I said to the cabbie. "I'll catch a ride with my friend."

Carl, the cab driver of the only cab company in town, didn't hesitate and pressed his foot to the gas pedal.

I watched the cab until I could no longer see the tail lights, and then I turned to stare in wonder at the house in front of me.

I saw the goats almost immediately.

They were in a pen set up to the left of the house, which was also where the dogs were laying down.

The moment I caught sight of them, they bolted up and started barreling towards me.

I braced myself, waiting for the inevitable impact of the huge polar dogs, but it never happened.

When I finally opened my eyes that I hadn't realized I'd closed, I saw both dogs, sitting on their rumps, staring at me.

Their tails were swishing in the dirt as they waited for some signal that I wasn't privy to.

Then I heard the whistle.

Following the sound, I saw the man I'd come there to see.

"You dropped your wallet," I informed him. "It was on the ground next to where your bike was parked."

"How nice of you to bring it to me," Apple drawled, sarcasm thick in his voice.

My eyebrows rose.

"I'm sorry if I offended you," I apologized. "It was never my intention."

He blinked, surprised that I'd willingly offered up an apology.

But then I said something stupid.

"It's not like I knew you were so sensitive about your name, or I would've never brought it up," I continued.

I could never just stop while I was ahead.

It didn't matter what I was doing.

Gambling and up a hundred and fifty bucks? I'd bet it fucking all and then promptly lose it.

Every single time without fail.

I was running ahead of schedule? I'd stop at the donut store before work. Then I'd get distracted by all the pretties and end up being ten minutes late.

That was how my life ran, though.

I was that person that never knew when to shut up. Add on top of that, I'd been drinking the entire night, and it ended up being *no bueno* for me.

"So, if you sent your cab away, how do you expect to get home?" He crossed his arms over his chest.

I looked at my watch.

"Actually…My brother and I only live about a five minutes' walk down the road from here," I pointed in the direction. "Didn't you know that?"

He shook his head.

“No,” he grumbled, obviously upset at that news. “I didn’t know that.”

“Apple!” An older man’s voice called from inside the house. “Where’s the coffee you bought?”

I raised a brow at him.

“Yeah, Apple. Where’s the coffee you bought?” I teased.

Apple’s eyes narrowed.

“Go home.”

CHAPTER 2

I'd call you a cunt, but you don't have the depth or the warmth.
-Apple's secret thoughts

Apple

She got all the way to the end of the driveway before I came to my senses.

Sighing, I looked at the dogs.

"Guard," I ordered, pointing at the chicken coop and goat pen.

The dogs left almost immediately, just like they were trained to do.

I, on the other hand, didn't want to do what I was trained to do.

I wanted to go to bed.

I'd had a long ass day and an even longer night thanks to some hunters that thought it'd be funny to destroy a bald eagle's nest.

Which meant I'd gotten to the club party late and then had to do shit duty.

I'd been hungrier than hell having missed breakfast and lunch, and the guys thought it'd be funny to make me eat last for my inability to show up on time.

I'd arrived about two minutes before the curly black haired

woman, belonging to none other than my biggest non-supporter in the entire fucking club, Ridley fucking Walker.

Turns out, my first erection in months came from his sister.

Fucking perfect.

"Well, you gonna let her walk home by herself or what?" My father barked from the doorway.

I flipped the old man off and started walking down the one lane dirt road that doubled as our driveway.

I turned the corner of my driveway, heading in the direction that I'd seen her turn, and stopped when I saw she wasn't anywhere in sight.

"Hey!" I called out loudly. "Where'd you go?"

Nothing happened for a long moment, and I used the time to walk even further.

Then a muffled curse, followed by the sound of leaves and sticks crunching had me looking to the side to see the woman coming out of the woods, buttoning her pants as she came.

"Sorry," she apologized. "I had to pee."

"I can see that," I replied dryly. "Come on. I'm tired and ready to go home."

She came in to step beside me, her hands buried deep down into the pockets of her jeans, making the thin material covering her pretty ass seem even tighter.

"Full moon," she broke the silence after a couple hundred yards. "I'm lucky."

"Why?" I asked.

"Because I walk nearly everywhere. A lot of times it isn't as light as this," she shrugged, her reply was brief and answered nothing.

I turned just my head to study her, seeing her long curls just barely touching the arch of her back.

"Why do you walk everywhere?" I asked snidely. "Don't have your license?"

I couldn't tell you why I was being such a dick. However, I'd spent the entire night with the girl and then she'd gone and said my name like it was a dirty word…just like her fucking brother.

She didn't answer.

Her eyes were settled on the road in front of us, making it known, without words, that she didn't want to talk about why she did all the walking that she did.

Touché.

I had my own touchy subject that I'd warned her off of already tonight.

I'd give her the change of subject.

"I don't date," she said suddenly.

My brows squeezed in confusion.

"Uh," I mumbled. "Okay."

We reached her door, and I winced when I saw the lights on inside.

"Your brother's gonna kick my ass you know," I told her.

"Why?" Her brows furrowed.

I snorted.

"A, because he doesn't like me. Two, because he doesn't like me," I explained seriously.

"My brother's suspicious," she amended. "And he doesn't hate you. If he hated you, you'd be treated like my other brother."

"And how's that?" I asked, crossing my arms over my chest.

"Like a common criminal," she licked her lips. "Ridley keeps him under surveillance, and he doesn't get to come around me, him, or any of the club members."

"Hmm," my mind started to race. "Interesting."

She nodded.

"He's not here," she informed me.

"Okay," I said, my eyes following the movement of her finger as she brought one manicured finger up to her mouth and bit lightly on the nail.

"Do I have to spell it out for you?" She rubbed lightly on her bottom lip.

I rebalanced my weight on both feet as I readied myself for whatever was going to come out of her mouth next.

I wasn't disappointed. It was quite shocking, to say the least.

"I want you to fuck me," she burst out.

She didn't lead up to it or anything, just blurted that shit out there.

Which might've been why I couldn't think of anything to say to that.

"I'm…" I hesitated.

"You're a pussy," she crossed her arms, brows raised.

My eyebrows lowered.

"That's certainly not what I was going to say," I informed her. "Which you would've known had you not interrupted me."

"Most people finish their sentences in a timely manner," she countered stiffly.

She was getting pissed.

Interesting.

"Desperate much?" I asked her. "You have to proposition guys that don't want you in an attempt to get what you want?"

Her mouth dropped open in affront.

"You're shitting me right now, aren't you?" She gasped, hurt evident in her voice.

"Yes," I lied, contrite. "But you surprised me is all. And I'm not a pussy."

"Well, what are you?" She sniffed primly.

"Honestly?" I hesitated.

She nodded.

"Yes."

"I'm trying to get into a club that my father thinks'll be good for my PTSD and anger management," I answered. "And to do that, I need to not piss off the members; for example, your brother."

Her mouth thinned.

"My brother's already let you know that he doesn't like you. What's sleeping with his sister going to change?" She bit out.

I paused, unsure how to answer that.

"Well…" on one hand she was correct. He wasn't going to hate me any less if I slept with his sister.

I *did* find her attractive.

Extremely attractive.

She was gorgeous.

And I'm not talking in a girl next door kind of way. I'm talking about a 'keep her locked down in baggy pants and a sweatshirt' kind of way and still beat the men off with a stick.

She'd be hell on the heart, that was for sure.

Her long, black curly hair came to about mid back, and her porcelain white skin seemed almost luminescent under the light of the moon.

She had long legs that looked fucking superb in those tight jeans she had on, not to mention the black Jack Daniel's t-shirt she was wearing, cut up in that fashion that women seemed to like now-a-days, was only accentuating her curves.

And what little denial I tried to hang on to by the tips of my fingers slipped away, leaving only one thing on my mind.

I couldn't pass this opportunity up.

Not after I'd been lusting after the woman for so long, even though she didn't know that.

"You really want this?" I crowded her so close that she started backing up out of reaction.

She licked her lips, and then nodded.

"Yes," she confirmed. "Or I wouldn't have brought it up."

"You know who I am?" He queried. "You're not intoxicated and asking for things that you shouldn't be asking for in this condition."

She laughed in my face.

"Oh, honey. Now you're just trying to think up an excuse to back out, aren't you?" She mocked me.

I reached for her wrist and yanked her to me, pulling her so hard and fast that she had no other recourse but to slam up against me.

"Does it feel like I want to back out?" I asked her, grinding my cock against her leg.

She licked her lips, eyes flared, and shook her head.

"Nope," she said almost casually, even though her breaths were coming in shallow pants, clearly showing me she was anything but not affected.

"What is it you want from me?" I pushed her, letting my breath play over her lips.

We were so close that the irises of her eyes looked like huge pools of liquid green, and when she went to lick her lips, her tongue brushed my lips.

My eyes flared, and hers seemed to absolutely melt, desire filling up those liquid depths.

"I want your cock," she breathed, leaning herself forward until our lips brushed. "But you already know that."

"Nothing else?" I asked.

She shook her head.

I smiled then and went to work on the button of her jeans.

The thing about our neighborhood was that we were in a fairly secluded area.

The Caddo River was a little over half a mile away from my place, which was at the end of the road.

There were only four other houses on this street, and Kitt's was the second to last one, next to mine.

Meaning, there was going to be no one else coming by here for quite a while.

I also didn't have to worry about her brother coming home, because I was supposed to be at the clubhouse early for a meeting.

The others were staying the night.

Me being the prospect meant I didn't get the opportunity to do that.

I was expected to leave late, be there early, *and* be on time.

Something that I'd already failed at today, but with this woman in my arms, at this moment in time, I found myself not caring quite so much.

She inhaled quickly when my cold fingers met the warm skin of her belly.

Her eyes showed no reluctance as I unbuttoned, then unzipped, her jeans.

And, all the while, her eyes stayed connected to mine, I let my fingers slip into the gap in her pants, nearly inhaling my tongue when I felt how wet she was.

The lips of her sex were drenched, and I knew instantly that this wasn't something that'd just started happening. She had to have been wanting it all night.

"How long have you wanted this?" I whispered, walking her back until her knees met the bumper of Ridley's truck.

She leaned back and bit her lip, letting me know without words what I'd already suspected.

My fingers delved between the lips of her sex, sliding down with little effort until I met her entrance.

A whimper escaped her throat when I plunged my middle finger inside.

My cock jumped at the way her tight pussy clutched at my finger, and I just knew that when I got my cock inside of her, it'd feel fucking divine.

"You want my cock inside of you?" I goaded her, curling my finger around to run the pad of my finger along the front wall of her sex.

She gasped and jolted, throwing her hips forward and towards me, urging me to continue.

I smiled and slowed my movements, watching her as she lifted her head in aggravation.

"Why'd you stop?" She snapped.

My eyebrows rose.

"Maybe because I'm trying to keep you from falling to your knees and taking me with you," I muttered, withdrawing my hand from her pants and bringing my fingers up to my lips.

I inhaled, smelling the sugary sweet scent of her essence on my fingers and nearly growled when she pushed my hand to my mouth.

I opened my lips and sucked my fingers inside, and nearly came when she leaned forward and took my thumb into her mouth as well.

I let my fingers go with a soft suck, and she did the same, staring at me expectantly.

Picking her up by the waist, I sat her on the truck's hood and grinned.

"Scoot back," I ordered.

She did and stopped when her entire body was directly in the middle of the hood.

"He's going to kill me," I muttered, grabbing a hold of the bumper that took up the front of Ridley's truck and lurched forward. "This would be easier if we went inside," I told her.

She laughed and started working her pants down her hips, taking her panties with them.

"Yeah," she agreed softly. "But where's the fun in that?"

I grunted and leaned forward, putting one knee on the hood and the other holding me steady on the bumper.

My mouth watered when she exposed her pussy to my gaze, and when she kicked her boots off, followed by her pants, letting both fall carelessly to the ground, I decided right then and there this wouldn't be the last time we did this.

Not if I had anything to say about it.

She may want just a one night stand, but I wasn't one to fool myself.

This, what we had, was explosive.

And the way my cock was raging right then, there was no way that once would ever be enough.

"Well?" She widened her legs and exposed herself to me.

The light of the street lamp that ran down our road, as well as the flood light that was lit on the side of her house, illuminated everything that Kitt had to offer perfectly to my needy gaze.

My cock felt heavy in my jeans as I leaned up and unsnapped them.

Pop-pop-pop-pop-pop.

My buttons went, one by one, until there was nothing left to undo.

My cock strained the front of my boxer briefs, pushing out of the gap in my jeans.

"You're sure about this?" I murmured huskily as I leaned over her.

She nodded.

"Okay," I pulled my cock out of my boxers and slid them, with the jeans, down my legs.

The moment my jeans were down, I shivered. It was March and already hot during the day. But at night, it was like it couldn't seem to figure out exactly what it wanted to do.

Which my balls took notice of when they were exposed to the elements

"God," she whispered. "Can you just fuck me already? You're like the slowest man in the world."

She shifted restlessly on the hood, her ass screeching when she tried to move without lifting her hips.

I snorted and pulled her down, uncaring that her skin hung and screeched across the hood as the friction of the two were rubbed together.

"That wasn't necessary," she growled breathlessly once I had her where I wanted her.

I leaned forward until my cock was touching her entrance and then thrust inside.

She gasped and bowed, her hair getting caught somewhere up above her head.

Neither of us paid any attention to it, though, as my cock was engulfed in her tight heat.

"Goddamn," I gasped shortly, watching where we were joined.

I pulled out and then thrust back inside, very aware of the fact that I was bare inside of her.

"You're on the pill?" I confirmed.

She shook her head, and I cursed.

When I pulled out, though, she shook her head and wrapped her legs around my hips, holding me still.

"Don't stop," she begged urgently.

This was one of those times where I should have realized that a woman like this didn't come without a whole slew of problems.

There had to be something that was keeping her from being with a man.

She could get anyone, and she'd chosen me.

I wasn't the most attractive man on earth. In fact, I was a broken mother fucker, and my beard left a lot to be desired.

But she wanted me, and I wanted her, and that kept my brain from working right.

Meaning, I should've pulled out.

That was what any normal person would do at a time like this.

Unprotected sex equaled babies, and I didn't want a baby. Not now, not ever.

Babies meant relationships, and there was no room in my life for a relationship at this juncture in time.

My cock, however, didn't care.

All I could manage to do was pull out only minutely, then thrust back inside.

Hard.

She gasped and strained her neck backwards, her legs going even tighter.

I squeezed her hip with one hand as I leaned over and planted the other hand on the sleek black hood beside her chest.

She smiled as she realized she'd gotten her way and started to pulse her pussy on purpose.

I saw stars, and it took everything I had not to rush my release.

"Motherfucker…" I breathed, bending down even further to pull her nipple into my mouth.

She moaned and placed both hands at the back of my head, holding me in place while she lifted her hips to take my cock.

My balls drew up, and I ground my pubic bone into her clit, hoping to help her along.

She gasped at the coarse feel of my pubic hair rubbing her sensitive clit.

"Jesus," she whispered. "How'd you learn to move your hips like that?"

I didn't bother to answer. She didn't really want to know that answer, anyway.

Not right then, anyway, with me pounding away inside of her.

She moaned and clenched me tighter, and I switched to the opposite breast, sensing the change in her.

And when her orgasm swept over her, I finally let go to chase my own.

My balls drew up and I came.

I emptied everything I had into her, and pulled out, watching as my release leaked out of her onto the hood of the truck.

"You're gonna need to make sure you clean this up well," I told her, tucking myself back into my pants despite the fact that my cock still throbbed.

She laughed, and I watched as even more leaked out.

“Don’t do that,” she whispered, sitting up.

I hopped down and tossed her the jeans.

She took the panties out of the leg hole and cleaned herself up, followed by the hood of the truck.

“Thanks for that,” she whispered, her feet going to the bumper.

She hopped lithely to the ground and I smiled as she strolled back into the house, naked from the bottom down, and slammed the door shut behind her.

I picked up her boots and tossed them onto the front porch, smiling as I did.

My night had turned around after all.

CHAPTER 3

In Texas if you yell 'The stars at night are big and bright' where someone can hear you, they'll answer with 'deep in the heart of Texas.'
-Proven Fact

Kitt

"There's a biker here to see you," I called as I came out of my room.

My brother, dressed fully in his sheriff's deputy uniform of brown paints and brown shirt, with the yellow stripe down the side of his legs, moseyed to the window and looked out.

"About fucking time," he muttered.

"What's about fucking time?" I wondered as I grabbed my jeans out of the laundry basket and slipped them on.

"We had a meeting today, and I asked him to follow me to work. He said he had to check on his pop first, and that he'd meet me here," he answered. "Did you know he lives just down the road from us?"

I buttoned my jeans and started searching for a shirt to put over my camisole.

"No, had no clue. How cool?" I lied.

"You know where my belt is?"

I pointed to the couch.

My brother grabbed his gun belt off the couch, where he'd left it two days ago when he got off shift, and belted it around his waist.

"Thanks," he muttered.

A knock sounded at the door right when I found a t-shirt.

Instead of putting it on, though, I walked to the door and swung it open wide.

Apple's eyes immediately went to my breasts.

I smiled.

See, that was one of the advantages of having no boobs to speak of. When you didn't feel like it, you didn't have to wear a bra.

Now being one of those times.

Apple's eyes never even lifted off my breasts, so I cleared my throat.

"Good morning, Core," I drawled, using the name he'd acquired during his time with The Uncertain Saints.

Apple's eyes slowly moved up the length of my body, stopping when he reached my eyes.

"Mornin'," he murmured. "Ridley in?"

I moved to the side to show Ridley shoving his face full of

powdered donuts.

"Hey!" I growled indignantly. "I was taking those to school with me!"

Ridley shrugged.

"Sorry," he lied, white powder spraying out as he did.

I sighed and pinched the bridge of my nose.

"Seriously," I groaned. "Fucking wonderful."

Ridley moved to the kitchen for a glass of milk, and just when I went to grab my boots that were outside on the porch, Apple pulled me until my back hit the door.

Then his mouth was on mine, his tongue plunging inside my mouth.

He tasted sweet. Like jelly or sugar of some kind.

But I lost the desire to qualify what I was tasting when he leaned into me and let me feel the length of his hard erection lining the front of his work pants.

His hat tipped back askew, and I moaned into his mouth when his cock started to grind into my pussy.

He ripped his face away from mine and dropped me to my feet, leaving me standing there, panting.

"What?" I gasped in confusion.

Then I heard my brother's clodhoppers banging toward us.

"Have you seen my phone, Kitt?" Ridley called. "I can't find it."

"Couch," my voice croaked. I cleared my throat and said more clearly, "Couch."

"Ahh, there it is. Thank you," Ridley said, shoving the phone into his pocket, picking up his keys off the floor next to the coffee table, and walked toward us.

"Why's your face all red?" he asked, pushing his way past me.

Apple had already stepped all the way down the porch steps to his bike, leaving me there looking utterly ridiculous.

Fumbling with the shirt, I pulled it off over my head and reached for my boots.

"Why are these outside?" Ridley asked.

My face flushed even more.

Last night was so not me.

In fact, it wasn't even in the same realm as the normal me.

"I don't know," I lied, following him down the steps once I got them pulled on.

Ridley stopped next to the hood of his truck, and his eyes zeroed in a spot.

"Nice," my brother pointed to the ass print that was on the top of his truck. "I hope you're practicing safe sex."

I nearly swallowed my tongue, staring at my brother like he'd grown a second head.

I certainly *wasn't* practicing safe sex.

Apple's eyes flared at the mention of safe sex, and his eyes went down to the butt print he'd had a part in putting there the night before, and his eyes smiled.

His mouth didn't so much as twitch, though, causing me to want to throw my cup of coffee at him.

"Can you give me a ride today?" I batted my eyes.

Ridley looked at me, then back at his bike, and sighed.

"Yeah," he replied stubbornly.

I wanted to laugh, but my brother knew better than to not listen to me.

Especially after the fourth time of having to come get me from work or school.

I smiled and skirted past Apple to get in the front seat of Ridley's truck.

Apple's eyes stayed on my butt as I climbed inside, and I felt the brush of his fingers along the seam of my pants before I scooted into the seat completely.

I tossed him a heated look over my shoulder, admiring his outfit.

He was in a tan shirt that the muscles of his arms bulged out of. A pair of hunter green pants that hugged his sexy ass to near perfection. A pair of black boots and a white cowboy hat finished off the ensemble.

He looked pretty snazzy if I did say so myself.

I opened my mouth to reply when a shiver raced up my spine.

My eyesight narrowed, and I breathed out shakily.

"I'm going to throw up."

CHAPTER 4

I accidentally punched myself in the face while trying to pull my comforter up last night. If that doesn't accurately sum up my day, I don't know what does.
-Apple to Ridley

Apple

I was nervous as hell to see her.

Why, I didn't know.

I was a thirty-five-year-old grown man, and no little woman like the likes of Kitt Walker should make me shake in my boots, but she did.

After the meeting at the clubhouse this morning, I'd been tasked to follow Ridley to work so he could consult with me on something he was having trouble with.

All the men knew I used to be a police officer.

I'd spent ten years as a beat cop in Los Angeles, California, and I'd burned out quick.

I'd moved back to Texas, after a particularly bad arrest, quitting the force to lick my wounds.

I'd started helping my father with his logging business and was applying for jobs here, in hopes that I would not get sucked into the black hole that was my father's business. *Again.*

After having little success, I'd moved onto a different field, thinking that continuing my career as a game warden would prove more appealing.

And mostly, it had.

About six months ago I'd transferred from West Texas to East Texas.

Ultimately, I enjoyed the shit out of my job.

It was fun.

What I didn't enjoy was being brought back into the shit that I'd left behind.

Meaning, I was not looking forward to going to Ridley's office and learning why he wanted me to follow him there. Getting drawn back into a police matter, even just as a consultant, was not on the top of my favorite-things-to-do list.

But I'd do it anyway.

In the months that I'd been prospecting for The Uncertain Saints, I'd found that I was sleeping better at night.

My headaches came less often, and I could breathe easier with them surrounding me.

I didn't think they had any idea just exactly what they were doing for me, but I was glad to tell my father he was right.

And the woman currently shaking her ass at me was putting all of that in jeopardy.

Because I knew, if Ridley realized I'd fucked his sister, he'd not be happy about it.

As one of the founding members of The Uncertain Saints, Ridley's wishes would hold more power. Would count for more.

And I needed another woman like I needed a hole in the head.

Seriously, if it didn't have to do with my dick, there wasn't anything I needed from a woman

But my dick didn't care.

It wanted Kitt Walker, and I had no say so in the matter.

"Hope you're practicing safe sex," Ridley finished off sarcastically with his sister.

I winced.

We hadn't done that.

And now I was sweating.

Although that might be due to the fact that Kitt kept swaying her hips in my direction.

Or the possibly because she had her tits hanging out of that shirt she was wearing.

My hand moved on auto pilot as she got into the truck, giving me an almost perfect view of her pussy.

My fingers lightly brushed over the seam of her jeans that ran along the length of her sex before my hand dropped back down to my side.

She smiled at me.

Then that smile quickly fell from her face.

Within seconds of that happening she looked at me and said, "I'm going to throw up."

But then…nothing.

Not a damn thing.

She zoned out, her face went blank, and her breathing became heavy.

"Kitt," I snapped my fingers in front of her face. "Hey. You okay?"

Ridley cursed from the other side of the truck.

"Is she looking at you?" He leaned over.

I looked at him, then back to her.

"No," I shook my head. "What's wrong?"

"Seizure," he said simply. "Give her about thirty more seconds."

My heart started to gallop in my chest.

"What?" I cursed.

"She suffers from seizures. She's lucky. These are fairly light to what she could be experiencing, according to her doctor," he answered, getting into the truck all the way and buckling himself in.

"Ugh," Kitt said not even ten seconds later. "Nasty."

"What's nasty?" I blinked. "Are you okay?"

"Yes," she answered. "And the metal. It makes me nauseous."

"I'm so confused," I shook my head and let her face go.

She smiled understandingly at me.

"Seizure. When I'm about to experience one, I get what's called an 'aura.' It is sort of like a premonition of things to come. Tingles rake up my spine and then nausea starts to roll over me. Then I don't remember anything that happens until I come back to myself a little while later. My mouth always tastes like metal."

I opened my mouth, then closed it again.

"Well, okay, then," I backed off. "Do you still want me to follow you?"

Ridley nodded.

"Yeah. I'll meet you at the station. Would you mind picking up some batteries from the supermarket on your way? Double As," he gestured absently.

I nodded mutely and shut the door to the truck, backing away so they could leave.

The nonchalance that both of them were exhibiting was quite disturbing. They acted like this happened all the time.

And maybe it did.

To them. To me, it didn't.

I was a goddamned mess!

She'd had a seizure! In front of me.

And now she was going to work like it didn't even happen.

My eyes followed the truck until I could no longer see it, then I got on my bike, started it up and drove to the supermarket for batteries.

Then I went to Ridley's office and waited for him outside.

He pulled in two minutes after me and parked, stepping out and looking directly at me.

"My sister's a grown woman," he mentioned.

I blinked but didn't say anything.

"I can tell," I murmured.

"So I don't necessarily care or notice who she does and does not fuck," he continued.

I closed my eyes, knowing instantly where this was going.

"I have my house wired," he pointed out.

I blew out a breath.

"And I really, really don't like seeing that you fucked my sister on my truck," he said casually.

When I didn't reply, he kept going.

"I expect it washed within the next day," he continued. "I don't like seeing my sister's ass print on the hood when I'm driving."

I nodded sharply.

"She's not fucked up," he leveled with me.

I looked up at him sharply. "I never said she was."

"You looked at her like she was a freak show," he stated.

I was shaking my head before he'd even finished his statement.

"I didn't look at her like she was a freak show. I looked at her in alarm, because my buddy used to have seizures; when he had them, they were debilitating. It'd take him over twenty-four hours to recover, sometimes more. It was just weird to see her act like nothing even happened," I explained.

Ridley's eyes held relief.

"Don't let me stop you from dating her. I may not like you, but that's because I saw," he pointed at me. "I know what you did."

I grimaced.

I had tried to cover it up.

In fact, I thought I *had* covered it up.

But I wasn't worried Ridley would tell anybody anything.

Aside from the other Uncertain Saints, I highly doubted he would ever mention this again.

"You got your head on straight?" He waited. "You're not going to freak out on my sister?"

I opened my mouth, then shut it, shaking my head.

"I think I do," I finally settled for. "Y'all are helping."

Ridley's eyes sharpened.

"What?"

His face was clouded in confusion.

"Y'all asked me why I wanted to be a part of the Saints a couple of months ago when I started prospecting," I cleared my throat. "What you just said—*my best friend*—he was the reason. On top of everything else. I just needed…something."

"That's not what you said to Peek," he said carefully.

Peek was the club president.

"It also wasn't a lie. Just not the total truth," I told him just as carefully.

"So you do have PTSD."

I nodded.

"And you've attempted suicide," he continued.

I looked up at him sharply.

"How?" I asked.

"Got a good man named Silas. He's a fucking genius at finding information," he answered. "That's how I found out about your best friend. And your hospital stays after you killed him. You still think about doing that?"

"Not so much anymore," I answered slowly, trying very hard not to be sucked in by the memories.

Ridley looked at me for so long that I wondered if this wasn't going to go a different way.

He surprised me, though, by nodding.

"I know why you did it. I'm not saying I'd ever do it the same way, but I know why. And I respect that. But you need to tell Peek exactly why you're here, or I will," he informed me.

I nodded, swallowing thickly.

I'd been waiting for this.

I'd always planned to tell them, but to just spout your every fault, failure and insecurity, was a fucking nightmare in and of itself.

It wasn't easy to tell someone something that they could later hold against you.

I'd intended to tell them everything, but it'd just been hard.

Too hard.

***

I drove to work on autopilot.

Today, I was working a new spot on the Caddo River, and I was curious as hell to see if my suspicions would hold water.

Duck season had ended the past weekend, and I'd assumed, yesterday, that everyone would realize that.

Seeing as this was my second duck season as a game warden, my first alone, I'd honestly never thought that anyone wouldn't know that.

I mean, there was a fucking rule guide.

So color me surprised when I arrived to run the river and found two men out duck hunting.

I'd given them a warning.

They were eighty something years old and had a stamp for the current year.

They also hadn't done any killing that morning, so I was lenient.

It was up to my discretion.

However, after I'd let them go, I'd seen them go up into a crop of trees and head to their house that was just off the main part of the lake.

Then, almost as an afterthought, I'd decided to do a little checking around about them.

What I'd found hadn't been good, either.

And after calling the old warden that used to run this particular stretch, I'd become more than slightly pissed.

In fact, I would classify it as being a lot pissed.

Those motherfuckers had played me.

McGraw had had quite a bit of shit to say about the pair, and the more I heard, the more solid my plan was.

I'd go to the exact spot I'd seen them at that morning, and if I didn't find them there, I'd keep looking for the little fuckers until I did.

After arriving at the station, I hooked up the boat to my truck, and then checked to make sure everything I needed was in the boat.

After a quick stop inside to check my company email and voice messages, I was off.

I arrived at the spot I'd found the two men yesterday, and was awarded with the sight of the two men.

This time, I caught them red-handed.

And I knew they knew that they were in trouble.

"Hello, gentleman."

Twenty minutes later, I had the two old men handcuffed on the seat of my boat. Their boat was tethered to the back of mine, and I was heading up river to the boat ramp.

The four birds that the men had killed were laying in evidence bags at my feet, and I was hot.

Not only had the men shot birds out of season, they'd also shot *protected* birds.

My eyes caught on Ridley who was waiting for me on the dock, his eyes blank.

I pulled up to the pier, hooked my boat to the dock, and headed to the two men.

"Get up," I ordered them.

The two of them got up and walked to the side of the boat.

Ridley and another young deputy I'd seen that morning, reached out and helped them out.

"Take them up to the cruiser," Ridley ordered the other deputy.

I grimaced, knowing it was coming.

"Two old men?" His eyes sparkled. "Really?"

I sighed and took the line off my boat that the men had been using.

After tying it off, I reached inside the boat and took up the weapons they'd been using, as well as the birds.

"Can you run this into evidence for me?" I asked. "And call someone to pick this boat up for me?"

The game wardens and the sheriff's office used the same evidence collection facility, meaning that there was no reason on earth Ridley should've denied me the help.

"What do I get in return?" He countered.

I gritted my teeth.

"What do you want?" I leveled with him.

He smiled.

And I knew I wasn't going to like his answer.

"Take my sister out on a date tonight," he ordered.

I narrowed my eyes.

"What if she doesn't want to go on a date with me?"

He shrugged.

"Then she'll say no."

I narrowed my eyes and wondered what his game was; but, in the end, I shrugged and went with it.

I was doing better.

Surely, one date wouldn't change my life, would it?

CHAPTER 5

If you have to force it, leave it. Friendships. Yoga poses. Relationships. Food. A fart. No matter what, that shit ain't worth it.

-Note to Self

Kitt

My belly rolled, and I wanted to cry.

I was about to go on a date with Apple. My first date in so long that I couldn't even begin to count.

Was it high school?

College?

No. I didn't actually finish a date in college. My brother had had to come get me because the guy was being a dick and wanted more than I was offering.

So I'd called him from the bathroom and waited there until he came to get me.

That was when I started giving my brother's number to anyone that asked for my number.

It was easier to not date, but there was something about Apple's insistence over the last two weeks that really had me breaking down and giving in to him.

"You're wearing that?" Ridley eyed me.

I looked down at my jeans, boots and t-shirt.

"Yes. Why?" I looked behind me as best as I could to check out my ass.

No, there was nothing on it.

"Because you look so…plain," he observed. "Can't you do your makeup?"

I touched my cheek.

"I put mascara on, that's about it. Why do you care how I look?"

"Because you come home whining about needing to do this or that differently. I'm just trying to make sure you get it right the first time," he teased.

I flipped my brother off, and his phone chirped with a text.

"Who is it?" I questioned when I saw my brother's smile.

"Some guy named Jason. You remember him?" Ridley murmured. I nodded, remembering him very well.

He was the toucher.

I'd stood next to him for all of ten minutes while we were waiting on his oil to get changed, and this man had been so unsuspecting.

I'd met him during my lunch break during classes yesterday and had immediately gotten that 'weird' vibe from him.

So what do I do when he asked for my number?

I gave him Ridley's.

At first, it'd just been to tease my brother, but Ridley knew how to take a joke and had turned it into a hilarious endeavor.

Meaning now whenever I met someone who asked for my number, I gave them to my brother.

Sure, it was cruel, but life was short, and I deserved to get a laugh every now and then.

"Core's here," Ridley said absentmindedly as he typed out a reply to whatever the man had sent to him.

I smiled and walked to the door.

"Why do you call him Core without him here, and Apple when he is?" I called out as I peeked out the window.

Ridley didn't reply until he was done texting Jason.

"Because I think it pisses him off," he replied.

"Why do you want to piss him off?" I continued, watching as Apple parked his bike beside my brother's and got off.

We were going to Arizona for the next four days. We'd drive there, stay the night, and then drive back. We'd also be stopping halfway in between at a hotel when the guys were tired of riding.

Ridley got up and turned off some lights, and I followed suit, catching the lights in the kitchen and my bedroom.

"You know," I said as I flipped the one in the hallway off. "It'd be easier, as well as cheaper, if you'd shut a light off when you left the room."

With the house dark like it was, I never saw him coming. Ridley grabbed me up around the waist and I screeched, flailing and kicking in response to the sudden movement.

My heart pounded in my throat as Ridley's laughter echoed in my ear.

I elbowed him hard in the ribs when a light from someone's flashlight shined in my face, causing me to shield my eyes.

"Damn, Apple. Is that a flashlight or are you happy to see me?" Ridley boomed as he put me down.

I pushed my brother away and walked towards Apple, an apology already on my face.

"My brother's a peckerhead," I enlightened him.

Apple's face transformed into a brilliant smile.

"I knew that already. Are you ready to go?" He grinned.

I nodded, moving to the front door and looking at my brother warily.

"I won't," Ridley promised, almost sensing my disquiet.

I breathed a sigh of relief and walked out the door that Apple was holding open.

"What was that about?" Apple wondered as soon as we made it outside.

"That was me making sure my brother didn't do anything stupid," I informed him.

"What does he normally do?" He took my elbow and guided me down the walkway to his bike.

I bit my lip as I watched him get on.

He offered me his hand, and I smiled as I took it.

"Helmet!" Ridley bellowed from the front door.

I winced and looked at Apple.

He smiled.

"We're just going down the road to my house," he answered, not nearly as loud as Ridley had questioned him.

"I don't care!" Ridley said rudely.

I patted Apple on the shoulder and mounted behind him.

"Go before he starts acting like an ass," I ordered Apple.

Apple did, and I clutched him around the chest and laid my head on his shoulder.

Ridley was still screaming at us as we left, and I waved, using my middle finger to do it.

Ridley had the decency to laugh.

Apple never got up over fifteen miles an hour as we rode the short way to his house, and I found myself annoyed that the ride didn't last longer.

Meaning I growled my disapproval.

"Did you just growl at me?" Apple questioned as he flipped the kickstand down on his bike.

I laughed.

"I wanted to ride longer," I told him, explaining myself.

He patted my thigh and got off the bike, which seemed to be a signal for the dogs to come over and greet him.

"Sit," Apple's smooth, deep voice growled out.

The dogs, all five of them, sat.

And they were all massive, white, humongous, polar bear type things.

"Jesus," I exclaimed. "These are freakin' huge. What do they weigh, two hundred pounds?"

"Big Poppa is the biggest and oldest. He's about one eighty. The rest trickle down from there," he pointed, indicating the biggest.

"Wow," I uttered. "That's more than me."

Apple's grin was almost contagious and probably would have been had his laughter not been at the expense of my weight.

"Don't even go there," I ordered him.

He held his hands up.

"So what has your brother done to all your dates that you feel you have to gather a promise from him to make sure he behaves himself?" Apple asked, taking my hand and guiding me through the dogs that still hadn't moved.

But they watched and wagged their long tails.

One such tail caught me on the back of one ankle, nearly throwing my leg out from under me.

Apple caught me before I could hit the ground, pulling me in front of him as he kept walking.

"Have you done that before?" I gasped on a breathless laugh.

Apple snorted.

"One or two times," he answered, looking down into my eyes. "You have to be on your toes around them. They're a little rambunctious when I allow them free time."

"You allow them free time?" I quivered.

He nodded.

"They're working dogs. That's what they love to do," he answered, sweeping his hands up over the farm.

I stopped and looked at it.

It was a big farm; I'd give him that.

He'd led me around the main house to the back of the house, where a large barn overlooked sprawling pasture land.

Cows milled about, eating grass in the back pasture while goats climbed on top of the small storage shed in the closer one.

"Are they okay up there?" I bit my lip worriedly.

"They are." Apple promised. "Goats like to climb, and they're escape artists. That's why I have that ten-foot fence up, to keep them inside."

I snickered.

"So where do the dogs go at night?" I turned to him. "Do they come in?"

"They patrol the pasture land for predators," he pointed to the cows. "We have about a hundred acres that butt up to our land and runs straight down this road until it hits the main highway."

"Your land is the one behind ours?" I asked. "Is it your cow that keeps trying to come into our yard and eat our grass?"

"The grass is always greener on the other side," he countered teasingly.

I snorted.

"Do you live there with your dad?" I asked him.

He pointed to the barn.

"I live there," he jerked his chin. "There's a one-bedroom apartment that the cow hands used to rotate in and out of each summer. It's mine now."

"That's kind of cool," I let my eyes linger on his lips. "Do you like it here?"

My eyes looked around the spread he and his father had, and I found that I quite liked it.

It was beautiful and peaceful, even if it did smell like a farm.

He shrugged.

"It's okay," he said. "At one point, I was so used to living in the desert, the thought of a tiny one-bedroom cracker box in California seemed large. Now this…this is paradise compared to both of the last two living situations I had."

I smiled and walked toward a fence where a white donkey with a splash of brown sat rubbing his head on a fence post.

"Does he bite?" I looked over at him.

He shook his head.

"No," he denied. "Donkey doesn't much like people, though. So don't get too close."

"You named your donkey, Donkey?"

He shrugged.

"Once you start having the amount of farm animals that we do, names become irrelevant," he added as he walked up beside me.

I could feel the heat of him all along my side, and I started to tense in anticipation.

But he did nothing more, only stood next to me for a couple of long moments.

"Are you hungry?" He cleared his throat.

I turned to look at him.

"What do you have to eat?" I asked. "My answer will depend on that."

He snorted and grabbed my hand.

"What kind of food do you not like?" He asked.

I pursed my lips.

"I don't like smoked ham, bone in catfish, taco meat with tiny pieces of onion in it, burnt toast, or crunchy peanut butter," I listed.

"Who does like burnt toast?" He wondered as he led me into the barn.

I giggled.

"My brother," I informed him. "Burnt food has become one of his major food groups."

"Why's that?" He wanted to know as he started up the stairs.

He held onto my hand, though, making sure I didn't fall to my death down the steep steps.

I snickered.

"I suck at cooking. Literally. I would love to learn how to prepare a proper meal, but I just don't have the patience for it. I always forget about it, even when I'm standing right there," I informed him. "Why don't these stairs have a handrail?"

"Because it's something I added after the fact, and I was so impatient to move in that I didn't wait for it to get finished completely," he answered. "After I moved in a few years ago, the builders refused to finish it, stating that I'd broken their contract. Hence, why I never got the molding or paint up either."

I looked around once we'd reached the top of the stairs and immediately understood what he was talking about.

It was beautiful.

One wall was made completely of glass that overlooked the back of their property. All you could see now was darkness, but I guessed the view would be absolutely beautiful during the day.

The entire area was an open loft type area at the top of the stairs.

Two sliding barn doors were slid all the way open, exposing the apartment to the barn down below.

One side of the room had a kitchen. There was a wall that came off the kitchen that I guessed housed the bathroom.

The other side of the house was his bedroom area, with the washer and dryer butted up against the railing that kept you from falling to your death.

"I'm sure," I said. "Did you have the barn built specifically for this?" I asked him, my eyes taking in the unfinished parts that he'd told me about.

“Yes and no,” he spoke. “My pop kept all of his equipment outside,” he pointed out the window at an old shack like structure that only had a roof and one side. “He had two tractors stolen and countless saws that he used for work. After the fifth such incident, I decided to build him a barn and a convenient place for the ranch hands to use. Then I decided to use it myself as a more permanent place to stay.”

“You didn’t like living with your dad?” I teased.

He looked at me seriously and said, “You don’t like living with your brother.”

I snorted. “Touché.”

“My dad’s not that bad. He’s just stubborn and pigheaded, and always thinks he knows better than me. He treats me like I’m still fifteen. Forget to pick up after myself one freakin’ time, and he blows a gasket.” He shook his head. “Forgets that I’m the one who does all the work now, and all he does is live there on the income that I bring in.

I blinked, surprised by the vehemence in his voice.

“Do I sense a sticky subject?” I winced.

He sighed and walked to the small kitchenette area.

“It is and it isn’t,” he amended. “A couple of years ago, my father had a stroke, and he became mostly wheelchair bound.”

“But he can walk,” I guessed.

Apple nodded, pulling out two bottles of water and walking towards me.

Once he reached me, he handed the ice cold bottle to me and grabbed me by the hand, guiding me to the couch.

It was pretty. Not something I would ever expect a man like Apple to have.

“It’s not my couch,” he answered my unasked question.

I snorted and turned my mirth filled eyes up to his as he took a seat next to me.

“What made you think I was wondering that?” I batted my eyelashes at him.

“Is there something wrong with your eye?” He leaned in closer.

I narrowed them at him.

“No,” I growled. “What would make you think that?”

He pressed right above my eye where it was now twitching.

I looked up at the massive thumb that was pressing the bone right under my eyebrow, then back to him.

“Your eye’s twitching.”

I sighed.

“I like your couch. I was just trying to flirt with you,” I informed him.

He grinned.

“I know. I just like giving you shit,” he provoked me.

I punched him in the belly and he moved out of my reach like a boxer anticipating the move.

“Sorry,” he chuckled. “It’s just nice to tease you. You’re a lot different from your brother.”

"I sure would hope so," I muttered, twisting the cap off the bottle. "Although, my brother would be just as happy to hear that as I am."

"Y'all don't get along?" He questioned, leaning back into the cushions of the pretty couch, his eyes on my face.

I shrugged.

"We get along okay. I won't be brokenhearted when he decides to move out," I informed him.

"What makes you think he's going to move out?" He took a sip of his water.

I sighed.

"Because the house is mine," I semi-lied. "And he needs to get a life."

He blinked.

"Why is he there then?"

I leaned forward.

"My brother doesn't understand boundaries," I began. "He doesn't get that I don't need him up my ass all day, every day."

"So you move out," Apple suggested.

I was shaking my head before he'd even got the words past his lips.

"It's my house," I informed him. "It should be my brother that should move."

"What makes it yours over his?" He turned his head to study me. "From what I heard, it's the house he shared with his wife."

"Well, we all shared it," I said. "Besides, my grandfather left it to me, even though we all love that house."

"Seems to me that that house means something to him. Maybe it holds the only thing left of his wife?" He guessed. "And maybe he wants to live with you."

Damn man logic.

I groaned.

"I don't really want him to move. Unless it's Sunday, and he decides he wants to stink the kitchen up with chorizo," I amended. "I just wished he gave me a little bit of privacy."

"You can come over here anytime you want. The code to get into the barn is 2-3-3-2," he said. "That'll open the doors. And if the top barn doors are closed, all you have to do is push them to the side and close it behind you."

I smiled then, a full-out, light-up-your-face, cheek-hurting smile.

"Thank you," I told him softly. "My brother can be a bit overwhelming sometimes."

He gave me a look that clearly said that he knew exactly what I was talking about.

"If you ever get under my brother's wing of protection," I promised him. "He'll move heaven and earth for you."

He looked at me like I'd just second guessed myself, and I suppose I had.

"I don't want to talk about it," I snapped.

He snorted and kicked his feet up onto the coffee table.

"I can make a frozen pizza or tacos. Which one do you want?" He looked at me.

I turned on the couch to face him completely. "Is that even a legitimate question?"

He shrugged.

"I think my taco meat might have bits of onions in it," he teased.

I stuck my tongue out at him.

"I want tacos," I chirped. "I'll take my chances with the onions."

Turns out, his taco meat didn't have any onions. None at all.

"This is good!" I told him forty-five minutes later. "You could totally make this for me every day, and I'd never complain."

He snorted.

"What's your favorite dessert?" He took another bite of his taco.

"I don't have one specific favorite," I informed him. "I have more like ten."

His eyes lit with fascination as I told him my favorites and all of the individual qualities that made them great.

Then I told him about my schooling and my job.

He returned the favor, telling me about his.

We sat that way over the kitchen table, telling each other about our likes and dislikes, our wants and desires, for well over two hours.

It would've gone on even longer, but the late hour was starting to show on Apple's tired shoulders.

So I made him take me home, even though he clearly let me know that he didn't want me to go.

But one thing was for certain.

Over good food and lots of laughs, I fell deeply in love with Apple Drew.

I knew as he was walking me back to my house, later that night, that I'd never, ever, be able to get free of him. Not that I wanted to.

There was just something about the man that intrigued me.

The butterflies in my belly started to take flight as he stopped me at the bottom steps of my front porch.

"Your brother's looking out the window," he sighed.

I turned to see my brother doing just that.

He waved at me, and I waved back before turning my back on him.

"My brother's a shithead. Have I mentioned that?"

Apple's face broke out into a smile and he lifted his hand to tuck a stray lock of my hair back behind my ear before resting the palm of his hand on my cheek.

"I had a good time with you tonight," he told me softly.

I leaned forward until my hands were resting on his abs.

"I had a great time, too," I informed him. "Thank you."

He grinned.

"I know it wasn't much. But I get off work at six, so I don't have as much time to do stuff in the evenings," he explained.

He seemed to hesitate before he said what he said next.

"Do you remember when I said I'd take you to Arizona with me?"

I nodded, the butterflies in my belly fluttering faster.

"Do you still want to go?" He asked, sounding almost hopefully.

I nodded again, this time with a brilliant smile on my face.

"Yeah, I still want to go," I promised.

His eyes lit up as he leaned forward and placed his lips on mine.

The beating on the window didn't deter us, either, as our tongues tangled.

His hands came up to frame my face as he took control of the kiss.

I moaned into his mouth as his tongue plunged deep, and his hips pushed me into the door at my back.

My leg came up to hook around his thigh, but he moved his face away from mine before I could get any deeper into the kiss.

"Sorry," he muttered.

It was then I realized he wasn't talking to me.

He was talking to my brother.

"Seriously?" I asked Ridley, looking over to where he was watching us through the open window.

CHAPTER 6

Adulthood is like looking both ways to cross a street only to get hit by a falling object. Unpredictable and headache inducing.
-Fact of Life

Kitt

My second date, which was to last all weekend, was officially about to start.

A wave of nausea rolled over me at the idea of being in the same room with Apple again.

Not because anything was amiss with Apple, but because I'd revealed some pretty personal details about myself on our date three days prior.

He'd done so as well, and then I hadn't heard a word from him.

So yes, I was very, very nervous.

The loud rumble of pipes had me rushing to find my pants.

"Ridley!" I yelled. "Will you bring me my pants out of the dryer?"

I heard my brother's groan of annoyance, and then the stomping of his feet as he walked away from the kitchen where he'd been eating a snack.

A few moments later a knock sounded at the door, and I moved the drapes away from my window to see Apple standing a few feet away from the entranceway, his back more toward my window rather than the door.

I knocked on the glass, a smile breaking out over my face when he turned and smiled at me.

Then his eyes trailed down my legs, and his smile got wider.

I rolled my eyes and dropped the drapes just as I heard the sound of my pants hitting my closed bedroom door.

"Thank you!" I yelled just as I heard him open the front door for Apple.

Snatching them off the floor, I closed the door behind myself once again and yanked the material up my legs.

Once up over my hips, I sat down and shoved my feet into my untied shoes, before standing and walking to the bathroom.

The pants were deliciously warm from the dryer, which was why I didn't notice that they were too tight until I tried to button them and couldn't.

"Shit," I groaned, looking down at my pants in dismay.

I looked at my bag where I'd literally packed it all the way full with all the clothes, supplies, and shit I'd thought I would need, and then back down to my pants.

Coming to a decision, I walked to the bed and flopped down backwards, then commenced trying to button them.

My fingers ached as I tried to suck in and button them, and I knew after about my tenth attempt that it was likely not going to happen.

"Ridley!" I yelled. "Come in here and help me button my pants."

He was my last hope.

If he couldn't get it done, I'd have to unpack some of my jeans, seeing as I'd packed the only ones I was willing to wear in front of Apple.

I was so engrossed in trying to get them buttoned that I didn't realize who had just come in my room until I heard the amused chuckle.

I looked up to find Apple standing in my door, watching me with an entertained look on his face as he watched me struggle.

"Now, if your brother moved out, who, exactly, would help you button your pants?" He batted his eyelashes, voice laced with laughter.

I narrowed my eyes at him.

"And maybe you need his help tying your shoes, too?" He continued, not realizing the danger zone he was entering.

"You're not funny, you know that, right?" I asked him.

He winked and walked forward.

"Your brother's in the bathroom. He said he'd be another twenty or thirty minutes because something he ate was 'tearing his stomach up'," he answered. "And I'm not sure he's able to help you right now. What do you need?"

I fell back on the bed in defeat, trying not to think about my brother's bowels and telling him I told you so. He should've never eaten the shrimp leftovers from last night. He knew what it did to him.

"I need help buttoning my pants." I pointed to my jeans.

His eyes fell on my pants, and the expanse of exposed belly I was showing.

"Is that right?" He stepped back, threw the door closed and locked it before prowling forward.

I swallowed convulsively as I watched his tight body, encased in faded jeans that hugged his body perfectly and a t-shirt that fit him like a second skin, stalk toward me.

"I only need help buttoning them," I informed him, watching him warily.

"Maybe we should examine the insides before we worry about the outside," he suggested, taking a hold of my jeans and pulling.

I held on to the waistband, meaning I came with them as he pulled.

That didn't deter him, though.

All it did was delay him, and not really that badly.

One second I was holding onto the waistband, and the next I was flipped over onto my belly and looking at the faded blue quilt that covered my bed.

"Apple," I gasped in surprise by the sudden movement.

"Yeah?" He rasped.

My hands automatically went under my chest to push myself up, and he got the chance he was needing, yanking my pants and panties down to my ankles all in one fell swoop.

I pulled my knees up under my body and lifted up onto hands and knees in disbelief, looking over my shoulder as I did.

"What are you doing?" I whisper-shrieked.

"What I should've done three days ago," he licked his lips. "I can't have you on the back of my bike for hours without having you again."

"My brother…" I hesitated as his mouth descended on my exposed pussy.

"Is in the bathroom; where he will be for a long time, according to him," he said. "If not, this is your house, too. He'll get over it." He swiped his tongue from my pussy entrance up, his tongue barely grazing my asshole.

"Holy shit," I breathed.

"And weren't you saying you wanted him to move out?" He continued his torture.

"Ummm," I hummed, my brain not comprehending the words that I wished to speak.

"What better way than to have loud, wall-banging sex?" He murmured between licks.

My answer was to pant out a moan.

"Jesus," I whispered. "What has got into you?"

He sucked my clit into his mouth and my eyes crossed.

See, I wasn't very used to oral sex.

The two sexual partners I'd had over my twenty-eight years of life had never been able to use their lips like that.

And his beard trailing on the inside of my thighs, brushing over my sensitive lips, was really doing it for me.

Everything seemed heightened as he circled my clit with that talented tongue.

"You smell good," he growled. "And the answer to what's gotten into me, is you. You've gotten into me. I can't stop thinking about you. Your laugh. Your smell. Your taste. Your sense of humor. The way your eyes light up when you experience pleasure. Fucking everything about you has gotten into me, burrowed deep under my skin and won't let me go."

My head dropped to the bed as his whispered words washed over my body.

My pussy clenched on air as I moaned into the quilt.

"You better hurry," I whispered. "I would hate to have to ride on your bike sated with you still hard as a rock."

He chuckled darkly against my clit.

"Oh, I'll hurry," he promised, getting up to the bed behind me and unbuckling his belt.

Something hard hit the bed, but my mind was too focused on the way his belt slapped against the inside of my thigh.

The cool metal of his belt buckle trailing along my backside.

Then I felt the warm, blunt tip of his dick pressing against my folds, running up the length, and I lost the ability to focus.

"You're so wet," he whispered. "My cock is already coated in your juices. The tip is glistening with you."

I moaned causing him to chuckle again.

A door banged from somewhere in the house and Apple decided to stop taking his time.

Meaning, when he lined himself up at my entrance, he slammed inside without further ado.

"God yes," I moaned, clenching my fingers in the quilt.

He growled.

My wood framed bed creaked with each thrust, but I couldn't find it in me to care with Apple's cock filling me up so full that I could barely breathe.

"Oh, god," I whispered breathlessly. "I'm already close."

"Come," he ordered. "Don't wait for me. I'll follow you."

I took him at his word, my eyes slamming shut as he pounded inside of me.

I let my hand sneak between my open thighs to find my clit, slowly circling it with one finger to give me that last little push that I needed.

"Fuck me," Apple ground out gruffly. "I can feel your pussy trying to swallow me whole."

I wasn't aware what my vagina was doing to his cock at that moment in time because my orgasm took hold of me, pulling me down into the depths of pleasure so deep and hard that I didn't even have time to catch my breath.

One second, I was urging it forward, and the next it'd grabbed a hold of me.

Vaguely, I heard Apple curse as his thrusts become erratic.

Wet splashes of come shot from the tip of his cock, bathing my insides in his essence.

My eyes slammed shut as stars burst behind my lids, completely taking over my vision.

And I heard the slam of a door, closer this time, and my brother said. "Do you have your clothes on yet? And where the fuck is Apple?"

I quietly laughed as Apple pulled himself out of me, leaving me feeling bereft as he did.

"Jesus, it's dripping," I whispered frantically.

Apple grabbed my pillow and ripped the pillowcase off, shoving it between my legs to catch his release that started to leak from my entrance.

"Thanks," I muttered dryly. "That's exactly what I wanted all over my pillow."

He shrugged unrepentantly and shoved his still wet cock back into his pants.

"I'm going out the window. Hurry up," he ordered.

"But my pants!" I gasped before he could leave.

He stopped and looked at me expectantly.

I smiled and wiped myself clean with the pillowcase, tossing it into the hamper by the door.

Once clean enough, I yanked my pants and underwear back into place and hurried to him, tripping on my shoelaces as I did.

He caught me before I could test out the padding in the carpet and righted me.

Then buttoned my pants, effectively cutting off my air supply.

“Thanks,” I wheezed.

He winked as he walked over and opened the window without another word.

I sat on the bed and tied my shoes as I heard the front door open and my brother say, “Where the fuck have you been?”

I didn’t hear Apple’s reply.

I decided to hurry, though, just in case.

Grabbing my purse and my bag, I ran out the door of my bedroom.

Upon seeing me, Ridley gathered his wallet, keys and gun and started across the room.

“Was it decided where we are stopping to eat yet?” Ridley asked as he pushed out the door. “I’m hungry,” he explained. “Kitt, lock the door.”

I rolled my eyes, but pulled my keys out of my purse and locked the door, even though my brother could’ve done it just as easily as I could.

“The last I heard was that we were meeting at the interstate and then going to find something after that,” Apple said as he offered me his hand.

I took it and walked down the porch steps, tossing my bag to Ridley as I went.

He let it fall to the ground, and I lost sight of him as I rolled my eyes toward the sky as I asked God for a brother who wasn’t such a shithead in my next life.

When I finally looked forward, it was to find my small bag with the minimal clothes I was allowed to bring sitting next to Ridley’s bike. The moment we got close enough, Ridley picked it up and launched it at Apple.

"Told her to pack light, but this is likely as good as it's going to get. Let me know if you can't fit it all, and I'll shove some in mine," Ridley offered.

I stuck my tongue out at him, but it was lost on him since he couldn't see it.

It wouldn't be light yet for another hour, and I was actually kind of happy for that.

I was nervous as hell, and my face likely showed it.

I need time to chill out before he saw me fully in the light of day.

"Sounds good," Apple replied.

I waited nervously beside the bike and watched as Apple shoved my bag into the saddle bag, nervously biting my fingernail as I watched his ass in the near darkness.

I offered him my purse next, and my pills shook as he took it from me.

I could almost feel the caress of his gaze as he looked at me questioningly.

Yes, I had to take meds.

A lot of them.

Well, not a lot. Just two, but I had to take them frequently throughout the day.

I had partial complex seizures, and they were mostly controlled through the meds that I took morning, noon, and night. And I'd thrown in my multivitamins as well as some ibuprofen just in case.

Luckily he didn't reply, and I was thankful—thankful that I'd get a reprieve in telling him about my episodes.

Once he'd gotten my purse into the bags, he got onto the bike and offered me his hand.

I took it, my smooth palm fitting easily into his rough one.

His hands were callused, and I thought maybe a scar covered his hand, but I wasn't sure.

My fingers grasped his tightly as I mounted the bike behind him, suddenly extremely nervous.

"You got her a helmet, right?" Ridley broke in, drawing my attention.

"Yeah," Apple rumbled. "Here."

I took the helmet from him.

It was plain black, and I smiled.

I was happy he didn't buy me anything girly.

I didn't do pink or purple.

Black was my color, and I would probably self-destruct if I had to put anything sparkly or pink on.

"Thanks," I murmured softly.

I pushed it onto my head, grimacing when my hair was pushed down.

"Damn," I muttered.

"What?" Apple asked.

"I curled it. It's gonna look like shit once we get where we're going," I groaned.

He laughed then.

I felt the rumble of it through to my core.

"Scoot closer," he ordered.

I did, moving until I was plastered to his back.

He didn't have to ask me twice.

I couldn't wait to feel his skin under me again.

"Wrap your arms around my belly," he instructed.

I did, bringing them to rest just under his ribcage and linking my fingers.

He chuckled, which made his belly contract.

"You don't have to do it so formally, darlin'," he informed me. "Just put it right here."

He moved my hands down until they were resting against his belly.

And I felt the imprint of his gun, the metal one, not the flesh one.

I hadn't realized that he conceal carried.

But I guess he was a game warden and all. No man I'd ever seen would willingly trudge in after armed hunters without one.

I knew my brother carried everywhere he went since it was not against the law for a Licensed Enforcement Officer to carry concealed, but it'd never occurred to me that Apple would.

"Ready?" He rumbled, patting the outside of my thigh, jarring me out of the contemplation of his gun.

"Yes," I squeezed him tighter.

I couldn't contain the excitement in my voice.

Honestly, Ridley was freaked way the hell out about taking me out on his bike.

What if I fell? What if I had a seizure, and he didn't know until I was on the ground eating pavement? What if some girl thought I was his woman?

Okay, that last part wasn't likely to happen.

Ridley was still caught up in his love for his wife and, honestly, I couldn't blame him.

His wife, Aerie, had been a good woman.

And I missed her dearly.

But my hurt was nothing compared to what Ridley felt.

Apple started his bike, bringing me back to the present time and out of Ridley's nightmares, with a sharp jolt.

Apple obviously thought he'd scared me with the loudness of his engine, but honestly, that was nothing new to me.

I was around bikes a lot, even though I never rode on them. I'd even ridden on his bike to his house on our first date. Though, I did have to admit it was only about forty seconds there, and forty seconds back.

I let him have his illusions, though, and tightened my hold on his belly.

It was uncomfortable with his gun there, so I lowered my hands until they were resting on his lap, leaning so far forward that I practically lay against him.

When he didn't protest, I stayed where I was and squealed slightly when he started off.

He laughed and motored in the direction of the interstate.

I looked to the back of me only once to see Ridley, and he lifted his hand in acknowledgement.

I blew him a kiss, one in which I knew he could see due to the headlight shining in my eyes.

I could practically feel the eye roll he sent my way.

Turning back around, I pressed myself closer to Apple settled in to enjoy my ride.

In fact, I enjoyed it for a long time…until I didn't.

I hadn't realized that riding for such long periods of time would make me feel so sore, but by the time we'd stopped for the last time at a hotel about six hours from Arizona, I was near to exhausted.

In fact, I was definitely at the stage of 'never wanting to get on that bike again.'

Annie, Mig's wife, looked over at me in commiseration as I finally put both feet on the ground for the first time in hours.

"Sucks, doesn't it?" she asked, rubbing her sore backside.

I laughed shortly.

"You could say that," I said as I walked bowlegged, completely ignoring the fact that I had a bag and a purse in Apple's saddle bags.

As much as I enjoyed being pressed up against him for the whole day, I decided that the next time we went out together, I'd make sure it was a shorter ride than twelve hours.

"Where are you going?" Ridley called as I continued past the front door of the hotel we were staying at.

"On a walk to work out some of my stiffness," I said, but most of the explanation was lost on the wind.

I didn't bother to repeat myself, though.

Instead, I kept walking until I hit the back of the building, stopping when I saw a super pool on steroids.

It was beautiful, too.

It was about the size of a public pool that most would find in their communities, such as the one we had in Kilgore.

This one, though, wasn't a boring square one like the one we had at home.

No, this one was exotic or something, that's all I could think to say about it.

Maybe one that'd be found in the middle of Hawaii.

It had a beach entry from the back of the building that led into a lagoon colored pool which fanned out on the sides.

At the far back wall was a massive cliff made of rocks the size of a small car, and a young woman with a bikini—about the size of a doll's—jumped off the cliff into the pool.

Her man, or who I assumed was her man, sat at the edge of the pool with a beer in his hand, talking on his phone.

Wasn't he worried about it falling in, or getting accidentally splashed?

And why wasn't he playing with his girlfriend instead of talking on his phone?

Seemed to me that people were too busy playing or talking on their phones instead of enjoying the life that was passing them by.

"Wow!" Annie gasped from behind me. "This is *awesome!*"

I nodded in agreement.

"Wish I'd have brought my suit," I said bemusedly.

"I have one you can borrow," Lenore, Griffin's old lady, said.

I turned to her, eyed her petite frame, and immediately shook my head.

"Honey," I said softly. "You're beautiful, but your suit would never fit my ass."

She laughed.

"Well, I have bottoms you can wear," Annie said. "And I know my sister brought extra."

"Brought extra what?" Tasha, another member's old lady, asked as she, too, joined the group.

She crowded in between me and the building, though, putting her extremely close to me.

I couldn't back up, or I'd risk backing into one of them, so I chose to stay there.

I wasn't used to having this kind of a conversation.

I had friends, of course, but none of them really did anything with me outside of school or work.

These ladies were obviously very friendly with each other, and I'd longed to be a part of their group for a long time now.

However, now that I was here with them, I wasn't sure what to do or say.

"Let Kitt borrow one of your tops," she ordered, touching Tasha's boob.

"Sorry," she apologized. "I only brought one."

"What?" Annie asked in surprise. "Why?"

Tasha's lip curled up.

"Because my man thought I didn't need more than one," she said stubbornly, crossing her arms over her chest.

"Well then, you can wear one of my bottoms, and one of Lenore's tops!" Annie clapped. "Problem solved."

So that was how I ended up in a pool with all the women.

The men were all still in their jeans, boots, t-shirts, and leather cuts.

They were crowded around a table with beers in their hands or on the table.

All except Apple.

He didn't have anything.

And his eyes were on me.

Or my boobs.

I couldn't really tell.

I blushed and turned my head back to Alison, Peek's wife, and smiled.

"Yeah, I think I like him," I admitted.

Alison grinned and brought her margarita up to her mouth to take a long sip.

"Thought so," she winked conspiringly. "He suits you."

I grimaced.

"I might actually have a chance with him, for once," I told her. "My brother's a real shithead with people that he deems as 'outsiders'," I explained.

"Alison, what are you doing?" Peek yelled out.

Alison turned to survey her husband, her brows furrowed in confusion.

"Swimming, why?" She called back.

Peek's eyebrow rose.

"Is that right?" He asked. "Come 'ere."

I loved Peek's accent.

It was absolutely intoxicating to listen to him speak in that Irish accent of his.

I just bet it sounded sexy as hell to hear him whispering dirty things in her ear while they were having sex, which was why I completely missed the fact that my brother had stripped down to swim trunks somewhere in between my ogling another woman's man, and then.

"Cannon ball!" Ridley screamed.

I was instantly drenched, even my hair that I'd hadn't planned on getting wet.

"You fucker!" I hissed at my brother, launching myself at him.

Ridley was a fast cocksucker, though.

He got away from me before I could even reach out and touch him.

One second he was next to me, and the next he was all the way across the pool.

I narrowed my eyes, then did the only thing that I knew would get him over there.

I let the tears loose.

See, I had a *gift*.

One that had served me well over the last twenty-six and a half years.

I let my lip quiver, followed quickly by a lone tear.

I also held my arm across my chest, pulling it in tight and crossing my other arm over it to make it look like he'd hurt me when he'd done it.

Sneaking a glance from my head lowered position, I noticed that Ridley had lost his smile.

"Aw shit," he swam towards me.

"I'm sorry, Kitt," Ridley apologized as he moved towards me.

"Did I hurt you?"

Everyone around us had gone quiet, and I smiled, knowing all of them would be witness to the smack I was about to lay down.

Luckily, my wet hair was hiding most of my face from everyone's gaze, meaning no one, not even Ridley, could see the smile that twisted up further and further the closer he became.

"Kitt?" Ridley murmured once he got close, his arm coming out to rest on my shoulder.

I waited until he was in perfect striking distance, then launched my entire body at him, hitting him in the belly like a battering ram.

"Ooof," he grunted as he went down, my body on top.

I gasped a full breath of air before I followed him down into the water, then immediately wrapped my arms around his head.

He started struggling then, but I held on like a fucking tick, even going as far as to wrap my legs high around his chest.

He burst from the surface of the water, gasping for breath and trying to shake me off at the same time.

I held on, being sure to dig my fingernails into the side of his head as I did.

"Owww!" He yelled, thrashing to get me off him without hurting himself further. "Get off me, you fat cow!"

I snickered as Ridley started to use every dirty name in the book on me.

Once he got too close to the edge and the rocks, I planted my feet in his back and shoved off him, swimming frantically to the side of the pool.

He was fast. Luckily, I had the advantage of necessity.

I was nearly at the far wall, and climbing up the steps, when he caught me.

I screamed and held on for dear life.

"Let me go, you accident!" I yelled.

The insult made sense to no one but me, and I snickered as he cursed at me.

"You know damn well and good I was planned," he snapped. "You were the accident."

"I may have been an accident, but I wasn't the reason our parents got married. If it hadn't been for you, I'd have been born in a castle like I deserve," I teased.

A thick, callused hand reached out and wrapped around my bicep, causing me to look up in surprise.

Then I grinned and latched onto his shirt and pulled.

Wisely, Ridley didn't continue to pull, otherwise my suit would've gone right along with him.

"Thanks," I gasped, smiling at Apple.

Apple winked and walked back to his seat, the whole front of his shirt covered in water.

I walked with Apple to the table that they were all crowded around, and would've taken my brother's vacant seat but he decided to come out of the water as well, leaving me with nowhere to sit.

But it didn't stay that way for long, because Apple caught a towel from the lounge from behind him and opened his arms.

I smiled and went to him, intending to take it from him.

He had different ideas, though, and pulled me down onto his lap before he wrapped the towel around my body and pulled me in close to his chest.

"Thanks," I said softly.

He rumbled a 'welcome' and went back to his conversation.

"What are you saying you know who did it?" Apple asked. "Why didn't you tell me this yesterday?"

"Because I just remembered," Mig said shortly.

Apple's eyes narrowed.

"This is a bald eagle nest. This is so far out of the realm of being okay to forget," he argued, moving his hands to form air quotes. "It's not even funny. What's the guy look like that you saw coming in?"

I watched the group continue the conversation, move on to others, and laugh occasionally for another forty-five minutes, at least, before I got uncomfortable.

Ridley was talking to Mig and Casten periodically about their office and a case they were working on, meaning they weren't paying that much attention to me and Apple.

Something I was grateful for, moments later, when I turned and repositioned myself.

I also exposed myself at the same time.

Luckily, the towel hid most of the flash from everyone but Apple.

The one who I thought wasn't paying any attention to me, seeing as he hadn't said a thing to me in nearly half an hour.

He was speaking to Griffin about goats, for some reason, but the moment my breast became revealed under my towel, he shifted the towel up so it covered me head to toe.

I would've said he hadn't even realized he'd done it, but his cock started to harden underneath me, telling me he most definitely *did* catch the slip.

I moved experimentally, shifting my ass on his lap and closing my eyes as I did.

If I accidentally made eye contact with anyone at the table, I might blush and reveal that I was having naughty thoughts.

I reached my hand down, letting it trail along his chest and abs, stopping when I reached the buckle of his belt.

He'd lost the gun that'd been there all during the trip sometime in between us changing and coming down here.

Meaning, I was thankful because it gave me access to his belt buckle once I managed to move the towel out from under our two bodies, bunching it up to the side so I could make it happen.

He didn't show any outward signs that he liked what I was doing, but boy was his cock hard.

So hard that I was scared to unzip his jeans in fear that I'd catch his cock on the zipper.

Just when I finally found the courage to unzip the zipper, he abruptly stood.

"Let's go get you into your hotel room and changed," he said. "I have some things I need to talk about tonight, and I want to make sure you're settled."

The abruptness of the whole scene had me standing and grasping at the towel that was still in Apple's grasp.

He held onto it, though, meaning I either let go or play tug o' war with him.

Needless to say, I knew when I was beat.

I didn't fight for something that I knew I wouldn't win, and that towel wasn't one of them.

So I let it go and started shuffling to my room.

But he didn't follow me up to my room.

He stopped me about halfway up the steps, grabbed a hold of my hand, and pulled me to a stop just inside of the stairwell.

"Stop," he said softly.

I stopped and turned to find him at the bottom step, me four steps above him.

"You're not coming?" I asked.

He shook his head.

"No," he said.

"Why not?" I asked.

He ran his hands through his hair and looked down at his feet.

"I have to tell the guys something, and I'll come back to the room and talk to you about it once I'm done. I thought about it the whole way over here, and I just have to get it off my chest before we take this even further," he said softly, looking up at me with sadness in his eyes.

I nodded mutely.

"You remember the room number?" He hoped.

I nodded again.

"Good," he uttered. "I may be a little later, but if I'm not there by nine, come get me."

"Where will y'all be?" I asked.

He pointed down the stairs.

"There's a bar in the lobby that you missed since you came in through the backdoor," he informed me.

"Okay," I breathed, shivering slightly.

He grinned.

"Get up to the room," he ordered.

I nodded again.

When neither one of us moved, he started up the steps until his face was even with mine.

"I think you need to go," he said. "Or I'll have to take you right in this stairwell."

I shivered again.

"They have cameras," I pointed to the cameras that were in the corners of the stairs.

He grinned.

"I don't mind if you don't," he teased.

I blinked slowly, then smiled.

Leaning down, I pressed a kiss to his cheek.

"Hurry."

His eyes flared.

"I'll see what I can accomplish," he said.

I nodded and turned, but his grip on my hips had me halting.

"Did I tell you how fucking hot you looked in this?" He asked.

My head dropped to my chest.

"No," I told him breathily, my nipples beading into sharp little points.

But before I could act on the need that was exploding through my body, he was gone, and I was left alone in a cold stairwell with only the smell of him to keep me company.

"Holy shit," I breathed. "The man's going to be the death of me."

CHAPTER 7

I'm trying to cut down on my fucking swearing. Let's fucking see how the fuck that fucking goes. Fuck.
-Text from Kitt to Ridley

Apple

"Well, you got us," Mig said as he took another shot. "Are you ever going to grow a pair and tell us why we're all here getting drunk, instead of out with our women?"

I was getting to that.

I just needed another drink first.

I held my finger up to the bartender, and he brought me my eighth shot.

"You're going to die of alcohol poisoning. How are we going to get your bike home without you to drive it?" Ridley sighed in exasperation.

I took the shot the moment the bartender sat it down on the bar top in front of me.

"It'd be helpful as fuck if you didn't push me," I said, bringing the beer that the bartender followed up with up to my lips and took a long swallow.

I wasn't even tasting it at this point.

I nearly chickened out and that was about the point where I started ordering the shots.

"Come on, boy," Peek said thickly, finishing the last of his beer. "I got a hot, warm, willing woman in my bed. If you don't spit it out, I'm just going to assume you're not going to and get to her."

I downed the rest of the beer, not stopping until the only thing left was the foam.

"Fine," I ground out, looking around the bar.

There was no one there, which worked well.

I wasn't about to tell them my deepest, darkest secret with other people around.

It was one thing to tell them, men I knew I could trust to carry my secret to the grave.

Others that weren't in the same lifestyle…who didn't know how fucking hard it could be for a combat veteran to acclimate to regular life after they'd done so much time in combat.

Normal people just didn't understand.

These men in front of me, though, did.

"I met my best friend in the Army when I was eighteen. We stayed with each other all through boot camp, training and then later, the Army Rangers," I started.

I saw Peek wince when he realized that something bad was about to unfold.

A man didn't have to drink eight shots of whiskey to tell a story unless it was bad.

"He got hurt," I continued. "We both did, but he was worse. We both came home, both of us fucked up as hell. Me with a head injury. My arm and back fucked. And him..."

I took a deep breath.

"He couldn't walk. Couldn't piss by himself, and he had seizures nearly once a week." I didn't look at Ridley when I said that. If I did, I would see the sympathy there, and I couldn't handle that right then. "He couldn't even get out of bed because both of his arms and one leg were blown off. He refused any and all treatment and help in getting his health and his life on track again after all that," I blew out a breath. "I started out better. Got a job on the Los Angeles police force once my head was deemed 'okay' and my arm healed. My head had supposedly healed, but the emotional damage wasn't healing, not at all. So, I lied. The longer I was home, the worse I got. I was violent. I got into fights and then blacked out and couldn't remember what I did the previous day." I shook my head. "It kept getting worse and worse until one day I made a deal with Stephen. One that was his idea, but I went along with it, and I shouldn't have."

My voice cracked as I said those last few words.

I needed another drink.

"It's okay, son," Peek said in his lilting Irish accent.

I closed my eyes.

Then reopened them and stared Peek in the eyes when I said what I had to say next.

"We both hated ourselves so much that we knew something had to be done. We made a deal. We shoot each other, that way it's not a suicide. Our parents would get our life insurance, and that'd be the end of it."

"But he didn't follow through," Peek guessed.

I gasped in a ragged breath, my chest so tight it hurt to breathe.

"Yeah," I choked. "That was one of those days that I could barely remember. I only know those few facts. That's all."

"So what happened?" Mig asked, having stayed silent this whole time, I'd nearly forgotten about him. I'd nearly forgotten about all of them being at my back.

"They thought I'd shot him out of self-defense," I explained. "I was still in uniform. I'd come to see him during my lunch while on shift."

"Damn," Ridley said.

I was sure he was thinking better of asking me to tell Peek now.

It was something that no man would ever want to divulge.

Not that he wanted to kill himself.

Not that he planned it out, and it would have happened if his friend had played his part and not chickened out when pulling the trigger.

I couldn't say the same for me.

I'd done my job. I'd pulled the trigger.

And I'd pay for that decision for the rest of my life.

Stephen haunted me in my dreams. In my waking moments.

There was never a time that Stephen *wasn't* there.

Until a certain lady had come into my life and had gone about changing my outlook on everything.

"So, how are you better right now?" Casten chimed in. "You're sitting here, not getting into a fights. What changed?"

I lowered my head and removed my hat.

The hat that I always wore, no matter what.

"Surgery," I twisted to the side and move my hair out of the way. "After I quit my job, the next day, blaming it on the job, I went in to see a doc about my episodes. He ran a CT scan and then saw the blood. It was a bleed so fine that it was missed by everyone but me. I knew something was wrong. I just wasn't willing to admit it."

"Fucking sucks, man," Peek rumbled. "Glad you told us."

He gestured to the bartender.

The bartender stopped in front of us once again, and Peek said, "Give me the bottle."

The bartender handed him the rest of the bottle of whiskey and walked to the end of the bar once again where the cute little redhead waitress was talking and flirting with him.

Peek poured me another shot.

"You still think about killing yourself?" Ridley asked bluntly.

I turned my gaze to his.

Then picked up the shot and downed it.

Fire burned down my throat as I shrugged.

"Not in the last two weeks," I told him honestly.

A slight gasp had me turning to see Kitt standing there, a look of shock covering her beautiful face.

And my belly sank.

Fuck me.

I'd never wanted her to hear that story.

Hell, I never wanted anyone to hear that story, but definitely not her.

And I could tell that she'd definitely put the timeline together.

It'd been exactly two weeks since I'd met her.

Two weeks and eight hours to be exact.

And it was the truth.

I hadn't once thought about killing myself in the last two weeks.

Everybody else heard the gasp as well as me, and they turned to see Kitt's ashen face.

"You need help to your room?" Ridley asked.

She bit her lip.

"No."

She wouldn't look me in the eyes, and studiously avoided them, letting me know clearly what she thought.

Ridley growled.

"You know better, Kitt," Ridley said through clenched teeth.

Kitt shrugged.

I turned around and presented Kitt with my back, shame pouring off of me in waves.

And somehow I knew that I just had a setback.

I was fucked, and not in a good way.

Needless to say, I didn't follow her back to the room.

***

Two hours later, I was about ten sheets to the wind and barely making it up to my room.

I fiddled with the door for about two minutes before a bleary-eyed woman opened it.

"You forget how to work your card?" Kitt asked with amusement.

I didn't answer her, only walked into the room and collapsed onto the bed.

"You want me to help you off with your boots and pants?" She asked laughingly.

I rolled over.

"Do your worst," I ordered.

My voice sounded rough. Way rougher than normal.

And I couldn't feel my face.

"You can't feel your face because you're drunk off your ass," Kitt said with a smile on her beautiful lips.

"Thank you," she whispered.

"For what?" I asked.

"For calling me beautiful," she whispered. "It's nice to hear it."

"You're the most beautiful woman I've ever seen in my life," I growled. "And don't ever let anyone tell you differently."

She blushed and that's when I realized all the lights were on.

"Why are all the lights blazing this late?" I asked, closing my eyes and letting her take my boots off.

"Because I was waiting for you. I wanted to tell you I understand."

She pulled my boots off, and they fell to the floor with a soft thump.

The hotel had excellent carpeting. Carpet that was so thick that it could possibly pass for a fucking extra bed—comfortably—if worst came to worst.

"You have a gun on your ankle," she whispered.

I wiggled my foot.

"I do," I looked at it, sounding surprised.

She giggled.

The Velcro on my ankle holster loosened and I smiled.

"You don't like guns?" I asked.

"No," she bit her lip. "It's not that. I just didn't realize you had them, that's all."

"Hmmmm," I drawled. "Interesting."

She moved up the bed and started working on my pants; my cock instantly got hard.

"I want you to fuck me," I told her. "Hop on my cock and fuck the hell out of me. Make me forget this shitty day."

I didn't see her face fall at the mention of my shitty day because I was already passed the hell out. If I had, I would've reassured her that it wasn't because of her.

Then I would've made love to her for hours afterwards.

Because that was exactly how the next couple of months went.

Misunderstanding after misunderstanding.

CHAPTER 8

Look me in the beard when I'm talking to you.
-T-shirt

Kitt

He was gone the next morning when my eyes finally opened.

I ate breakfast by myself, too, seeing as all my medication had to be taken with food.

Even my brother slept in.

The next two days I barely saw Apple.

Each time I tried to stop him and talk, he ignored me, made up an excuse, or plain old left without listening to anything I had to say.

The drive back was terrible.

Where before I'd enjoyed the entire time, albeit being uncomfortable, now I couldn't help but know with absolute certainty that Apple didn't want me riding with him.

But he'd brought me here, and he wouldn't leave me to find my own way home.

Ridley also didn't have the seat on the back of his bike that would allow me to ride with him; so, here I was, stuck in between a rock and a hard place.

The moment we pulled up in front of my house, he stopped only long enough to make sure Ridley and I didn't need anything, and then left without another word or glance back.

"Give him some time," Ridley said, drawing my attention away from Apple's tail lights.

I looked over at my brother, and then I gave him the time he needed.

***

The first day I saw him, once we'd gotten back, was at a birthday party.

He was working the keg, as well as the grill, and he was laughing and joking around with Mig and Annie like he'd not just ripped my heart out.

Not intentionally, I was sure.

But he'd done it, nonetheless.

No, he hadn't said anything mean to me.

What he had done, though, was look through me as if I didn't exist.

And when I tried to talk to him about what had happened, he looked at me, let me explain that I didn't judge him, and then walked away without another word.

So I was wondering what I was doing here.

I'd hoped by giving him a week to cool down and to think about what had happened, he'd be able to think rationally about this, and us.

But I was wrong.

It was exceptionally apparent that he wanted nothing to do with me, especially when he wrapped his arm around some girl that I'd never seen before.

He laughed at something she said and then leaned his head down to whisper something in her ear.

And that was enough for me.

Dropping my drink into the trash still-full, I walked out the back door and around the side of the house.

I'd have gone out the front, but that was where the party was being held since it had a bigger lawn than the back.

And there was a bounce house. *For the adults.*

So yes, they needed the room.

But it also meant I wouldn't be able to leave for a while.

So I walked to the dock and down it, stopping when I hit the end.

Sitting down, I picked up the cane fishing pole that was sitting on the doc, then stood back up and walked to the trees to look for a worm.

I hit pay dirt when I found the Catawba Worm Tree.

Picking off a few succulent morsels, I walked back to the fishing pole, hooked a worm onto the line via the tiniest motherfuckin' hook I'd ever seen, and tossed it out there.

It wasn't five seconds later that I caught my first fish, a tiny little Sun Perch that was the size of two of my fingers.

After removing him from the hook and tossing him back in the water, I flicked the pole back out and smiled when I felt another tug.

This went on for a good ten minutes before I felt like someone was watching me.

I didn't turn around.

I knew who it was.

And if he wanted to watch, then more power to him.

I wouldn't be talking to him.

We stayed like that for a long time. So long that I didn't even realize how much time had passed before the cool afternoon turned into a chilly night.

"You gonna sit there all day?" Apple asked me.

I nodded, not answering.

"You're wearing shorts," he said.

I nodded again.

I sure was.

But that was because today was a nice seventy-five degrees, despite it being in the middle of January.

Something warm wrapped around my shoulders, and I turned to look at Apple.

But he was already walking away, and I could tell he didn't want me to follow him.

And not having the courage to go after him, I let him leave.

Our visits continued like that.

We'd see each other, exchange a few words, and then go back to acting like neither existed.

I'd just about given up hope that he'd ever felt anything for me at all…especially when his act continued after two months.

But then the beginning of the end happened, leaving both of us reeling.

CHAPTER 9

I'm always disappointed when a liar's pants don't actually catch on fire.
-T-shirt

Kitt

Two months later

I woke up on the floor alone in my house.

My school books were scattered around me like I'd tossed them up in the air just to see where they'd land.

And my head hurt.

As well as my shin, jaw, and tongue.

I got up, carefully, and made my way into the bathroom.

Everything hurt.

Even my teeth.

I saw exactly why everything hurt a couple of minutes later when I got a good look at my mouth.

"Ugh," I said. "This is just great."

My front tooth was broken off, and the only thing left was about half the tooth.

"Fucking perfect," I said, drawing a deeper breath and closing my mouth.

Grabbing a four by four gauze pad from the medicine cabinet, I secured it with some medical tape and walked to my phone that was laying on the floor.

The first person I called was the dentist, because priorities, you know?

I followed that one up with two calls to Ridley's office, receiving a promise from his secretary that she'd tell him as soon as he got through with his 'very important meeting.'

Rolling my eyes, I grabbed the keys to Ridley's truck and walked out the door.

The fact that I was driving meant this was pretty dire to me.

I'd gotten used to the fact that I shouldn't be driving, but there was no way in hell I'd ever get a cab to take me across two county lines to the dentist.

Three hours later, and the fine new owner of a veneer for a front tooth, I made my way outside and up two blocks to the hospital.

No, I wasn't thinking so clearly.

Had I been, I would've gone to the hospital first. Not to mention I wouldn't have driven at all.

The first person I saw was a man about my age with a beautiful beard in gray scrubs.

"How can I help you?" He asked.

"I think I had a seizure," I blurted.

His eyebrows rose.

"You think?" he asked.

I nodded.

"Name?" He continued, shrugging it off.

"Kitt Walker," I said.

"Date of birth?"

The questions continued until he got to my explanation of what happened.

"When did this seizure happen?" He looked at me.

"Ummm," I hesitated. "About three hours ago I guess?"

"You guess?" He spoke carefully.

I nodded.

"Uh-huh," he said, turning back to his computer. "If you'll just go have a seat in the waiting room, I'll get someone with your shortly."

I followed his directions and went to the plastic seats, choosing to go to the very end of the hall to where there was the least people coughing and crying.

I'd been sitting for over an hour and a half when I was finally called back.

At the same time my phone buzzed.

I pressed ignore as I walked to the pretty nurse that was holding a chart against her chest.

"Kitt Walker?" She asked.

I nodded.

"Follow me back," she gestured with a clipboard, leading me not to the ER entrance, but a side door.

"We're taking you to the minor," she explained when she saw my questioning look.

I nodded and went along.

"Can you tell me what happened?" She pointed to the bed.

I nodded and held out my hand for her to take my blood pressure, then recounted the last couple of hours. Conveniently leaving out the part about me getting my tooth fixed first.

Priorities. I had them.

"Do you have a history of seizures?" She questioned as she pumped.

"Yes," I grimaced. "I've had partial complex seizures since I was eight years old."

She blinked.

"What medications do you take?" She continued.

I handed the list of medications that I took and then said, "If you wouldn't mind, I need to answer this before my brother sends out a search party."

She nodded and took the list.

"I'm going to enter this into the computer and come back to draw some blood, okay?"

I nodded and answered.

"Where the hell are you?" Ridley asked with a shout.

"At the ER," I explained. "I fell and hit my head."

"It looks like you've trashed the living room," he growled. "And there's blood on the floor. Do you not think that warrants a telephone call, Kitt?"

I pinched my eyes shut and tried to count backwards from ten, but my brother had a way of getting under my skin.

"I'm sorry," I said with false sweetness. "Next time I have a problem like this, I'll be sure to clean up before I head to the hospital. And as a FYI, I did call. Twice. And I texted. Your lovely secretary answered and informed me that you were in on an important meeting."

"I was eating lunch," he grumbled. "And I came home to see if I could get you to wash my shirts. Two people spit and pissed on me today. I've gone through my two spare sets of clothes, meaning I have nothing to wear for tomorrow. Guess you can't do that."

"Guess you'll have to figure out how to work the washing machine by yourself, big brother. I'm not quite sure how long I'll be here," I told him truthfully.

"Shit," he growled, sounding annoyed. "I'm going to have someone drop me off there and I'll drive you home, but I need to go to court. Are you sure you're okay?"

I rolled my eyes.

We'd been there, done that. I knew the protocol. It'd be at least a couple of hours now, anyway. He had most likely until a little after five before I needed to be picked up, and the courthouse closed at four thirty.

"That's fine," I said. "I'll be…"

"Ms. Walker?" A man's voice cleared from the doorway.

"Gotta go, bro. Love you," I said quickly, turning my attention to the cute doctor in front of me.

Something about him looked familiar, and I didn't realize just what it was until he introduced himself.

"I'm Dr. Drew. The nurse said you had a seizure today," he read from his chart.

Shivers raced down my spine at hearing that voice.

But it wasn't his voice. It had to be his brother's.

I studied him as he asked me questions.

Absently, I answered them, giving my full medical history while I studied his face and body.

He looked a lot like Apple.

Eerily so.

Where Apple had blonde hair that leaned toward more strawberry blonde, this man didn't. There was no questioning that this man was a redhead.

And he had tanned skin, exactly like Apple.

It was weird looking at him. I didn't think I'd ever seen a redhead with tanned skin before.

"What's the date of your last…" Dr. Drew continued.

"Are you related to Apple Drew?" I blurted, interrupting his questioning.

His eyes, the same blue as the man I was comparing him to, smiled.

"Yeah," he said. "Cousin."

Ahhh, that made sense.

I would've thought that they were brothers, but cousins explained the resemblance as well.

"I thought so," I said. "What was the date of my last what?"

He blinked, surprised at the abrupt switch of topics.

I shouldn't have bothered asking him.

Apple was still ignoring me, and even now, two months after whatever that'd been in the bar happened, my heart still ached. It was harder than hell to think about, and any time I slipped and thought about all the fun I'd had with him, and then the sudden cold shoulder, my heart raced and an ache formed in my chest.

Meaning I so did not want to talk to this man about his cousin.

"Last date of your menstrual cycle," he repeated.

I blinked, confusion furrowing my brows.

"I don't know," I admitted. "I don't have regular menstrual cycles and never have. But I think the last one I had was right before I started the semester, which would be in January."

"It's March. So you'd guess about two months?" He surmised.

I pursed my lips, shrugged, then nodded.

"Yeah," I said. "That sounds about right."

"What were you doing when the seizure started?" He studied me.

I winced.

"School work. In particular, I was reading about a case that we're working on at school tomorrow," I explained.

He nodded.

"Alright," he murmured. "I'm going to hook you up to the monitor, and we'll see how that looks. I doubt that we'll find anything since you seem to be fine right now. From here, I would suggest you follow up with your regular doctor."

I nodded, knowing that was going to be the stitch.

"And I'll get your cut sewn up," he said, standing up to peel the gauze back that I'd stuck to it earlier. "Looks like it'll take about two or three stitches."

"Doctor," a nurse said from the door. "Here are the labs."

The doctor held his hand out for them.

"Will you bring me the suture kit so we can sew her up?" He looked at the nurse. "Also, I want to go ahead and get some pain meds for her to take home. Can you go get me…"

He rattled off some letters and numbers, as well as a name that I didn't quite understand.

But that could be because of the man that arrived at the nurse's station about five feet from my door.

He leaned over and said something to the nurse, and the nurse pointed towards me.

"But doctor," the nurse said. "The meds you just prescribed can't be prescribed to pregnant women."

Apple, who'd turned and started forward towards me, froze at hearing those words.

His eyes locked on mine, and they practically lit with an inner fire.

My heart, which had already been beating about ninety to nothing at the sight of him, took off like a rocket into outer space.

Jesus. *Christ.*

Fifty awkward minutes later, I was holding my discharge papers and a picture of my unborn child.

An estimated nine-week old fetus.

And Apple was at my side.

He led me to Ridley's truck, and I didn't complain when he strapped my seatbelt on for me.

Didn't say a word until we were pulling up in front of my house.

Shutting the truck's engine off, he got out and walked to the door.

"Thanks," I muttered, pushing the door open before he could.

I caught a hold of my purse and slid it over my shoulder, then tried in vain to move around the large man.

"Excuse me," I said tightly.

"Kitt," he growled, and just that one word, on his lips, made my control break.

"I never knew…" I said. "I swear I didn't mean to."

He caught me up in his arms. "It's okay."

"No," I cried. "It's not."

"It'll be fine. We'll figure this mess out," he promised.

I stiffened in his arms, pulling away and swiping at the tears pouring down my cheeks.

"Mess?" I said carefully.

His eyes studied me just as carefully.

"Kitt," he said slowly.

I brushed his hand away.

"Me and my mess don't need you."

With that I walked inside, completely missing the devastation that broke out over his face.

***

One day later

I left the doctor absolutely terrified.

I'd first seen my OB/GYN to confirm what I already knew.

I'd next seen my seizure doc, who'd removed me from my medication and put me on a different one.

One that was safer for the baby.

Sweet baby Jesus.

What had I been thinking? I wasn't a dumbass. I knew how babies were made.

However, I'd been hearing for years that the medication I was on practically rendered me infertile.

And I'd just once wanted to feel normal.

Why was that so fucking hard?

And then *this* happens.

My eyes went down to the paperwork in my hands.

Do not take this medicine if you are considering becoming pregnant.

Cleft lip. Heart problems. Genital malformations. Brain defects.

Jesus Christ, what had I done?

CHAPTER 10

Can you see the 'fuck you' in my smile? I put it there just for you.
-Kitt to Apple

Apple

I watched her walk out of the hospital, her fourth visit this month, and wondered if I'd ever work up the courage to talk to her.

The one and only time I'd tried she'd completely shut me down.

Which I suppose I deserved.

I laughed humorlessly. No, there was no supposing about it. I did deserve it. Immensely.

Even more, I deserved to be shot for getting her pregnant in the first place.

Had I known then what I knew now, I wouldn't have touched her at all.

I never wanted her to know those dark secrets. People looked at you differently. And I never, ever, wanted to see that look on her face as she looked at me that night after she'd found out what I'd done.

God, man. I spoke to my best friend. *What a state I'm in. If you were here, you would've slapped me upside the head by now and showed me just how stupid I'm being!*

I spoke to my best friend a lot. He was sort of my voice of reason during my trials of stupidity.

Or when I didn't think I could make it through the day.

Those days were coming less and less lately, though. Thank God.

"What are you doing here?" A soft, feminine voice asked.

I turned to find Kitt standing directly behind me. How'd she'd gotten there, I didn't know. She must've walked around the parking lot, seen me, and then doubled back.

All while I was talking to my imaginary friend.

"Nothing," I lied.

She stared at me.

"You're full of shit," she said. "What are you really doing here?"

I shrugged. "Making sure you got here alright."

She narrowed her eyes.

"Why didn't you just offer to take me if you were going to come anyway?" She challenged.

I stiffened. "You know why."

"No," she denied, stopping me before I could get on my bike. "I don't know why. Don't you think if I did, I wouldn't be so confused about this? About us?"

I sighed.

"I committed the greatest act of blasphemy by killing my best friend. If anyone ever found out, I'd be prosecuted, sent to jail, and tortured every day of the rest of my life because I was once a cop," I challenged her.

Her eyes widened.

"Yeah," I said. "I can see you're getting it."

She shook her head.

"Wait," she said urgently.

But I didn't wait. I couldn't.

Not with the way her eyes held pity…and understanding.

No, not right now.

Maybe next week. Maybe next week I'd have the courage to talk to her.

Maybe next week I'd be able to go inside.

***

Two weeks later

I opened the door of the clubhouse and grimaced almost immediately.

Not because anything was amiss, but because the woman that wouldn't get off my mind was standing there, talking to all of the women.

"Oh, good!" Lenore, Griffin's wife, cried. "We need you to take us to the store."

"What store, and why?" I asked warily, trying to keep my eyes off of Kitt while I addressed Lenore.

It was tough, seeing as Kitt was standing next to Lenore, and Lenore paled in comparison to Kitt.

Kitt's hair was down today, flowing down her back.

She was wearing a tight white shirt, and I could clearly see the outline of her new pants. One's that I'd seen her buy last week, even though she hadn't seen me.

Her face was free of makeup, and her eyes were on me like I was the last breath of air in the middle of a raging inferno.

"The grocery store," Annie answered, throwing her jacket around her shoulders. "We're going to cook brisket for the party tomorrow."

I blinked.

"You called me over here to tell me you needed a ride to the store?" I asked.

They nodded.

All except Kitt, who was staring at the two women on either sides of her like they were crazy.

And they were.

"Y'all realize I was at work, right?" I asked them.

Kitt winced.

"Griffin and Mig told us to call you if we ever needed anything. And we need a ride," she replied defensively. "We've had too much to drink."

I pinched the bridge of my nose.

"Well," I said. "How about you wait until you sober up and then go?" I suggested. "I have to go back to work. Lose my number unless you actually need something."

I caught Kitt's eyes on the way out, and I swear I saw laughter there.

I'd just made it down the stairs to the under house parking that was underneath the clubhouse when Kitt caught up with me.

I knew she would.

"Apple!" Kitt cried once I'd mounted my bike. "Wait!"

I opened my eyes and stared at her with a bored sort of attachment.

"Yeah?" I asked.

"Could we…is it okay…can we have a," she cleared her throat. "I'd like to talk to you, if you have the time."

My lips thinned. "I don't."

Her eyes narrowed.

"You don't even know what I have to say," she muttered, crossing her arms over her chest.

The move tightened the white shirt she was wearing, and my eyes immediately zoned in on her belly, reminding me just why I needed to stay away from her.

For her sake…and the kid's sake.

They didn't need anything like what I had to offer in life.

Destruction was about all I had to give, and I didn't want to destroy someone like Kitt.

She'd suffered enough; she didn't deserve to suffer more.

"I know I was called away from work to a stupid errand that was ridiculous," I said. "And I know I would most likely still be at work if Lenore hadn't called and said there was something she needed help with concerning you."

"You came because you thought something was wrong with me?" She asked with a small smile covering her face.

I grinned at her and started the bike up with a throaty growl.

"Yeah," I said. "Now, if you'll excuse me, I have a different area I'm working today and I'm trying to cover that one and mine."

She frowned, and was just about to say something, but I revved the bike up and drowned out whatever she said.

I left with her staring longingly after me, her heart in her eyes.

The feelings she dragged out of me, though, I easily squashed back down with the look she gave me the night she heard I killed my best friend.

No, there wasn't going to be any her and me.

That I could promise her.

***

"Where's your sister at?" I asked Ridley over the phone one week later. "She's late for her appointment."

Ridley cursed. "Hold on. There's someone trying to drink and drive."

While I was waiting for him to get back to me, I sat down on the seat of my bike and glared at the front entrance of the hospital.

Kitt's hospital visits were once a week at an OB/GYN's office in Marshall and once every two weeks at a specialist in Dallas.

I went to every single one, and this week she was late.

Normally, she made them at the same time every day. This week, she was either late, or she wouldn't be having an appointment. Both of which I highly doubted.

"What is with that look on your face," Kitt broke in, startling me.

I jumped up, completely ignoring the fact that Ridley sounded like he was getting his ass kicked over the other end of the line and turned to stare at her.

"You're late," I accused.

She shook her head.

"I'm not," she disagreed. "I made it later so I knew you'd be able to get here in time."

I blinked.

She smiled.

"I was here in time for your normal appointment," I told her.

"I know," she shrugged. "But this way I get to talk to you before the appointment. And I can try to convince you that you'll like going."

"How do you know I'll like going?" I countered.

She rolled her eyes.

"You're driving me nuts," she insisted. "Come on."

She didn't have to pull my arm very hard.

I went, *willingly*.

I wanted to. I wanted to know how my child was doing.

And it actually scared the absolute crap out of me to know that, one day, I'd have a kid running around out there in the cruel world we were a part of.

She held my hand as she hurried towards the door.

Then stopped and turned back to the car we'd passed on the way inside.

It was a cop.

I recognized him from somewhere, but I couldn't quite put my finger on it.

"I've got to tell him that you'll drive me home," she said, turning to go back to the man in the car.

Mr. Officer rolled down his window, listened to what she had to say, rolled his eyes to me, and then said something back to Kitt.

Kitt shook her head as she said something to him.

The man looked back over to me and seemed to come to a decision before he nodded once, rolled the window up in Kitt's face, and started the car.

"What's one of your brother's deputies doing driving you here?" I asked her once she reached my side again.

Kitt took my hand, and the man who started to drive away stopped and glared at me.

I glared back, and clearly sent the message that Kitt was mine.

She may not be mine in the actual sense, but the woman was carrying my baby. It wouldn't matter if he had her, either. If I wanted to fuck her life up and claim her, she'd be mine. She wouldn't be able to resist.

But I wouldn't be able to do that.

Not now. Not two weeks from now. Never.

"I'm seventeen weeks," she said.

My eyes widened. "That many already?" I asked in alarm.

That left how many more? Twentyish?

Jesus Christ. She was literally almost halfway done!

Holy fuck!

My belly started to sour as I thought about a brand new kid coming into this shitty world.

A world that was rife with war, debt, famine, and laziness.

I never wanted to bring my kid into this world in the first place. I would be a shitty ass father.

A man that thought about killing himself until he met the baby's mother.

A man that *had* killed his best friend.

A man that had killed so many men in his lifetime that I would probably pay for it in my afterlife.

I was literally the last person on earth that deserved something so innocent.

So pure.

"What floor are you going to?" Another woman that was overly pregnant asked.

I turned my eyes to her, and then said, "Fourth floor." At the same time that Kitt replied with "Fifth floor."

The woman pressed both the fourth and fifth floor, and I eyed Kitt with confusion.

She waited until the woman got off at the third floor before she said, "I have a surprise for you."

Brows furrowed, we ignored the doors when they opened for the fourth floor and got out on the fifth.

It opened up into a large waiting room that looked like it was the central hub for multiple offices.

We went to the one that was labeled as 'Baby Vision.'

"It's not a psychiatrist, is it?" I asked jokingly.

She eyed me.

"Do you need a psychiatrist?" She eyed me.

I nodded.

She snorted.

"We could write a book together about all of our experiences. I'd bet it'd be a bestseller," she teased.

My heart started racing at the idea of telling anyone anything about my life.

It'd been hard enough telling the boys.

Telling anyone else, let alone having people read my experiences, was terror inducing.

"I…" I started to say, but stopped when Kitt went up to the window, leaned against the counter, and thrust her back out to stretch it.

"Hi, Kitt," the woman behind the counter greeted her by name. "You ready for today?"

Kitt nodded enthusiastically. "I am."

"This the daddy?" She asked, taking a long hard look at me.

Kitt looked over her shoulder at me, then turned back to the woman with a smile.

"It is," she confirmed.

The woman, Ann Marie, her nametag read, smiled and stood up.

"I'm glad you were able to convince him to come," she said. "You ready?"

Kitt nodded emphatically.

"Most definitely," she promised.

"Alright," she opened the door that led to the back entrance. "Did you have your pop today?"

Kitt laughed.

"Yes, I had a coke today," she promised.

The two ladies shared a secret laugh about something I wasn't privy to, and walked back towards a back room.

It was more than obvious that Kitt came here a lot. Enough that the two had an inside joke, even.

I felt out of place.

My eyes took in every single thing in the entire place, finally settling on the couch with a plethora of pillows mounding it.

There was also a table set up next to a computer with about eight million buttons on it.

And it was then that I realized what was going on.

But before I could fully back out of the room, both women grabbed me by a hand and pulled me to the couch that was directly in front of the biggest flat screen TV I'd ever seen.

"Today's the gender scan. We usually do this between eighteen and twenty weeks, but since Kitt's going to be gone to Dallas next week for some testing for her seizures, we're going to go ahead and do it today," Ann Marie said.

I looked over to Kitt sharply.

That was the first thing I'd heard about her going to Dallas for a week.

I would've asked her about it, too, but she quickly changed the subject, bringing my attention straight back to the screen in front of me.

"We get to see whether we're having a boy or a girl!" She rubbed her hands excitedly.

I gritted my teeth and looked at the screen, trying hard to make my heart stop pounding so hard.

It was a stupid thing to try to do.

I couldn't control my body's reactions, which had gotten me into trouble in the first place.

"Okay," Ann Marie said. "Let's get started."

I left the appointment an hour later, promising to myself that I would make each and every appointment until the baby—*my baby girl*—was born.

Even the ones in Dallas.

Why, you ask, did I start wanting that now?

Because I noticed a pattern.

Kitt only had seizures after she had a long, exciting day.

And if I could help prevent that in any way, I would.

I'd already noticed she'd quit school.

Not that I'd had a problem with that.

She had, and I felt bad.

Whatever was going on with this pregnancy was quickly taking almost every single freedom she had, and replacing them with fear and uncertainty.

And I'd do just about anything to take away that fear in her eyes.

Almost anything.

I wouldn't give her me.

She may think she could handle my fucked up self, but she'd be wrong.

CHAPTER 11

I set my alarm early so I have time to lay in bed and be sad that I have to get up.
-Text from Kitt to Ridley

Kitt

28 weeks pregnant

My eyes fluttered open, and I smiled at seeing Apple so close.

I leaned forward, pressing my lips against his, and sighed in contentment.

Then the position I was in slowly became apparent.

“What…” I started to say, realizing I wasn’t wearing any pants.

“Sorry,” Apple muttered. “Didn’t know what else to do.”

I wanted to throw up.

“What happened?” I croaked.

The door to the house creaked open signaling Ridley’s return, and Apple got up to go.

“Don’t leave!” I pleaded, my hand shooting out to wrap around Apple’s wrist.

Apple pulled his hand away gently.

"Don't worry. He won't know I was here," Apple promised.

I blinked in surprise.

"I don't care that my brother finds out that you're here or not," I snarled. "What I care about is you," I shot back.

Apple's eyes narrowed. "Then why do you keep asking that man to go to Dallas with you instead of me?"

I blinked.

"Because you were working, as well as Ridley and the rest of the Saints. What did you want me to do? Call a cab to take me the entire way?" I asked him.

Apple shrugged, not bothering to answer. He knew the answer was the same. I couldn't call a cab. I also didn't have anyone that could take me to Dallas every week. All of my friends and family had lives that kept them busy during the week when I had my appointments.

"You could've scheduled it a day when I could take you," Apple suggested, a hint of annoyance in his voice.

My lips thinned and I stood, bringing my blanket with me to wrap around my lower half.

"I did," I told him. "But you got called in, remember? At least that's the excuse you gave me."

"I also asked you to change the appointment to the day before or the day after," he shot back.

I sighed.

"You can't just reschedule an appointment in Dallas," I told him. "This one was made about four months ago. I have a recurring slot every week. If I cancel, there'll be another lady willing to take it that has to drive double the distance. Trust me."

Apple scowled and sat down on the bed.

Bending over, he slipped both feet into his boots, then stood once again.

Gathering his phone, keys, wallet, gun and drink from the bedside table, he looked down at me.

I really wish he'd been leaving my bed under different circumstances. I really hated that he only came to see me when I was sick, in trouble, or I had an appointment.

There was always a reason for him not to delve too deep under the surface, and I hated it. He used them as excuses to never talk about him.

I'd known the man seven months now, and not one damn time had I learned anything personal about him.

What I had learned about him was not even from him.

I'd met his father all of one time, and that was only because they'd delivered a package to my house that was addressed to Apple, and I'd hand delivered it in hopes that I'd get to see him.

Apple hadn't been home, but his father was.

His father that was in a wheelchair and had obvious stroke impairments.

And I'd wanted to introduce myself to him so badly, but I'd held off, knowing Apple wouldn't like me insinuating myself into his life like that.

But I was at a loss as to what to do.

I felt like I was left spinning, with no way to stop myself when it came to him.

"Make sure you call me to let me know you got there and home safely," he started toward the door.

"Apple," I rasped softly. "Why do you even care?"

I winced almost as soon as I said it.

I should've never just blurted that out there.

Apple's shoulders stiffened, and he turned around to stare at me almost blankly.

"Because my child's inside you," he said somberly. "It's the one good thing I've ever made in my life, and I'll protect it with everything that's in me."

"What does that even mean?" I asked him, my heart hurting for him. "Why won't you just talk to me? I'm here. I'll listen, and I'll never judge you."

He smiled sadly as he backed toward the door.

"You already have," he muttered. "You just don't know it yet."

I stared at the closed door after he left, sadness practically leaking out of my every pore.

I felt utterly defeated, and I didn't think I could do this anymore.

I physically did not have the ability to keep up.

My belly jumped, and I threaded my hand under my shirt, rubbing my hand over my belly where I'd felt the movement.

And I came to a decision, knowing it was the right one.

I'd try until I no longer had breath in my body.

Because not only was Apple the father of my baby…the little life inside of me that gave me so much love even when she wasn't even born yet. But also because Apple deserved it. And my baby did, too.

***

"And what did he say when you told him about going to Dallas with another man?" Ridley asked with a roll of his eyes.

"That I should make sure he drives the speed limit," I snorted, really cutting into my steak now.

Well, more like massacring it.

I wasn't in a good mood.

Why, you ask?

Three words.

Apple fucking Drew.

"Told you that would backfire," Ridley mumbled helpfully.

"Then why'd you let me do it?" I hissed.

In truth, I did it, just like I did it every week, in hopes to garner some sort of reaction other than boredom out of Apple.

It was as if he was just existing.

He'd go to my appointments, then leave in a matter of moments once they were done.

He'd see me home, then he'd be gone.

Although he didn't actually leave.

That I realized pretty early on.

He wasn't sneaky about making it obvious that he was watching me.

Any time I actually acknowledged that he was out there, though, he would leave.

Which meant I didn't engage him in conversation in any way.

When he wasn't at work, doing something for the club, or asleep, he was watching over me.

I would say it was sweet if it wasn't so fucking annoying.

The man was a stubborn, pigheaded fool.

And I didn't understand him a goddamn bit.

I'd been able to finally rip the story from Ridley after getting him drunk, and I couldn't see a goddamn thing wrong with what he did.

Don't get me wrong, I never condone violence.

However, I also don't feel like a man should pay penance for something that likely wasn't his doing in the first place.

Apple was taken advantage of by his friend. A friend who'd never looked past his own grief to see what his death would do to Apple.

Needless to say, I was more than willing to make the first move, but every time I got close, Apple would retreat.

So as to not destroy what little I was able to build, I gave him that space.

But that didn't mean I wasn't going to try to entice Apple into giving me what I wanted, which was him.

“It worked,” I said. “He came to talk to me.”

“No,” Ridley countered. “He came to yell at you.”

I snorted and turned back to the dinner that I was eating.

It’d been eleven weeks since the gender reveal, and I was officially in the third trimester of my pregnancy.

And I looked like it, too.

My body was really starting to show, and everything that used to fit didn’t anymore.

“Whatever,” I grumbled.

“He also held you for about four hours after your episode, although he doesn’t realize I know that,” Ridley snickered.

My face flushed.

I didn’t want to think about that.

Except the idea of what Apple had had to do today was gut-wrenching.

“Kitt…” Ridley said, recognizing the color on my face for the embarrassment that it was. “You need to get over it. Hopefully this is only for a short time longer, and then you’ll kick these seizures.”

I shrugged, knowing he was likely telling the truth.

Hell, my own doctor had even said that once I had the baby and I could go back on my regular meds, and when the hormones that were throwing my system out of balance finally evened out, that I’d likely not have another seizure.

That didn't make it any easier to deal with in the now, though.

"What do you mean you saw him hold me for four hours?" I startled. "Weren't you at work all day?"

He smiled sheepishly at me.

"What'd you do?" I asked warily.

"Nothing that you wouldn't do if the positions weren't reversed," he said. "How do you think I got Apple here while he was working?"

I hadn't thought about that.

I'd noticed he'd been in his work clothes earlier, but I hadn't thought to ask him how he was able to be here with me and not get in trouble.

"He follows me constantly," I told him. "Why else would he have been here?"

"No," he shook his head. "I have the house wired for sounds and video."

I blinked, surprised by what he'd just said.

"You *what*?" I repeated, still not comprehending the magnitude of what he'd just told me.

"Come on," he said, pulling my hand, and consequently me, to the living room.

He pushed me down onto the couch and turned to stare at me, his arms crossed tightly over his chest.

"I only did it for your own good, remember that," he ordered, handing me a TV changer.

I took it, then looked up to find him changing the input on the television.

And suddenly I was looking at about five different views of everywhere in the house.

The last one in the bottom corner had me staring at the television, with a remote in my hand.

"You…what…how…why?" I stuttered.

"I have to work, Kitt," he explained. "But I can't work and know that you're here, possibly dying. So I installed the camera, and I have someone monitoring it almost 24/7."

I closed my eyes.

"What about today?" I asked. "Do they turn it off when someone comes to help me, or do they keep watching?"

My face was a flaming ball of misery.

I knew the answer even before he answered it.

"Keep watching," he said. "That's what they're paid to do."

I blew out a shaky breath and brought my hand up to angrily swipe at the tears that formed to roll down my cheek.

"I wish you would've told me," I whispered. "Now I just have one more person privy to the fact that I have to have medicine shoved up my ass to get my seizures to stop."

He sighed.

"You have a medical problem, darlin'," he told me gently. "No one, not even me, has a problem doing what I have to do to make sure you and my niece stays okay. Okay?"

I laughed humorlessly. "How did Apple even figure out what and how to do that, anyway?"

It'd happened four times now in the last couple of months, me waking up Apple's arms around me, and each time I'd known he'd had to do that for me.

It was kind of hard to miss.

I didn't lose hours of time without it having to happen.

My brother. Apple.

Who was next? The rest of the club members?

I'd literally die if that ever happened to me. Literally die.

"It's either that, or you have to have a caregiver. Which way do you want it to be?" He asked.

I glared at him.

"You know which way I'd prefer it," I said selfishly. "Get over yourself."

He sighed.

"You want me to show you how it works?" He changed the subject.

I looked at the TV, then back to him, before shaking my head.

"No," I tossed myself back against the couch. "I'd rather know that someone's not watching me masturbate. Learning how it works doesn't let me have that disillusion anymore."

Ridley winced.

"That's never been my intention," he promised.

I shrugged.

"Is this like the Life Alert?" I asked. "If I fall, will a hot fireman come and save me?"

I might, or might not have, sounded a tad bit hopeful.

But I knew before he answered what he'd say.

We didn't have a fire department. We had a volunteer fire department, and most of the volunteers on the department had jobs. My brother could get here just as fast as one of them could.

Or, apparently, so could Apple.

Meaning I was well and truly screwed, and someone on the end of the Life Alert line, someone was privy to my every coming and going, literally.

Yes, my life sucked.

I knew it.

Ridley knew it.

Apple knew it.

Hell, I wouldn't be surprised if the guy at the corner gas station knew it at this point.

CHAPTER 12

I'm not sure if the doctor called me a beast, or told me I was obese. I'm going with a beast.
-Text message from Kitt to Apple

Apple

Four weeks later
32 weeks pregnant

I watched her cry for the fourth time that day through her bedroom window, and I came to a decision.

I would do whatever I had to do to make sure she didn't suffer anymore.

Anything.

This was pure torture, watching her cry her heart out.

Coming to a decision, I got off my bike that was directly in front of her house and made my way to her window.

I didn't bother with the door.

That'd take too long to get to her, and I couldn't stand one more single second of her crying.

I made a mental note to have a talk with her about not locking her window as I climbed through and walked directly to her.

She was crying so hard that she didn't even hear me come up until I spoke.

"Why are you crying?" I asked her.

She hiccupped and rolled over as much as her belly would allow.

"There…there…there's a bug," she whispered.

I blinked.

"What?" I was confused.

She nodded, hiccupping.

"Somewhere. It's on the floor. It crawled across my pillow and woke me up from my nap. It touched my face," she whispered brokenly.

I tried very hard not to laugh.

I really did.

But the way she was looking, absolutely terrified, had a smile breaking out over my face.

"It's not funny," she whispered. "And I have to pee!"

I tried to wipe the smile off my face as I walked in the direction she'd indicated.

"What kind of bug?" I asked, looking around the room.

"A big one," she sniffled, a little more clearly this time.

"Where'd you see it?" I continued.

"On the wall," she hiccupped. "Above the TV."

I walked to the wall and started to move things out of the way to look under them, all the while I felt Kitt's gaze on my back, burning a whole with the intensity.

"Why are you here?" She whispered.

I stopped and turned, leaning my backside against the dresser that held her TV.

"I don't know," I admitted. "I'm just…tired."

"Tired of working?" She guessed. "You do work a lot. That's all I ever see you do."

Because it keeps me from thinking about nothing but you.

Something crossed over her face. Hope and fear mixed in with reluctance.

"That's not why you're tired, is it?" She asked, sitting up and letting the blankets fall down, exposing her thighs to me.

I licked my lips, then moved my gaze back up to her face.

"No," I answered honestly. "I'm tired of staying away from you, and I've decided that maybe you can forgive me and give me a second chance."

Her head turned to the side in confusion.

"What are you even talking about right now?" She squinted. "There's nothing to forgive you for. You've done nothing wrong."

"I've killed a man," I snapped.

Her eyes softened.

"So what?" She snorted. "According to what Ridley told me, what I understand is that this happened at a time when you weren't of sound mind, Apple. You don't even remember doing it."

I relaxed slightly.

"I have memories of being there," I told her. "I just don't know why I did it. Even when I was at my worst, I still didn't have the urge to kill anyone or anything other than myself."

My thoughts were about a thousand miles away, so it never occurred to me to hold my tongue and keep my darkest thoughts from her until I spilled everything that I never wanted her to hear.

"I see it—*him*—in my dreams," I whispered, eyes going far away to latch on to a memory that never let me loose. "You were the only thing that calmed those demons. Then you looked at me like I was a speck of dust on your brand new shoes, after you heard that I killed my best friend."

Kitt's hands on my arm had me turning to look at her, the threads of my constant haunting dissipating as she did.

"I never, ever looked at you like that!" She insisted. "I would never look at you like that. What makes you say that I did? I never even heard you did that, and when I did finally figure it out, you weren't even there!"

"You didn't hear me tell them?" I asked.

She was shaking her head even before I finished.

"Then why did you look at me with that disgusted look the moment I turned around?" I asked.

Her brows furrowed as she thought back to that night so many months ago, then understanding dawned.

"My brother," she said. "My brother was eating a donut with jelly in it. He had taken a bite, but you had said something and he'd immediately spit it out straight onto the floor. It looked like a gory mess. I was looking at him like the disgusting freak that he is. And when my brother caught me at his back, he was scolding me for creeping up on him. He hates it when I scare him."

My stomach knotted.

"You…motherfucker," I breathed. "Goddammit."

"You're telling me that you spent nearly seven and a half months away from me all because of a look you thought I gave you and didn't?" She screeched, getting up onto her hands and knees.

Then she went a step further and stood up, thrusting her belly out and placing her hands on her hips as she glared.

"You. Fucking. ASSHOLE!" She finished on a scream.

I stood up and looked at her warily.

"I thought…" I started.

She held up her hand to stop me, freezing my apology and subsequent explanation before it even started.

"You can save your bullshit," she said. "Get out of my room."

I started forward.

She held up her hand again.

"You need to leave," she insisted. "Before I start freaking out on you and say things *I* don't mean."

I nodded.

"I'm sorry," I whispered.

She shook her head and pointed to the window.

"Go," she ordered softly.

Stomach churning, I decided not to press the issue just *yet*.

With emphasis on yet.

Because I'd wait for her to calm down, then I'd do what I had to do to fix what I'd broken.

"Okay," I said, getting up and heading toward her.

Her eyes watched me, shuttered with pain and anguish over what I'd done to her.

"I'm sorry," I murmured, pulling her into me.

I liked the way she felt in my arms, so soft and warm in all the right places.

She didn't put her arms around me, but I could feel that she wanted to.

Her arms partially lifted, and her head tilted back to look at me.

Instead of them curving around me, though, her hands went to the side of my shirt and clutched it tightly.

"You need to give me space. When I'm ready to talk to you, I'll tell you, okay?" She trembled.

I leaned forward and placed my lips on her forehead, lingering as long as she'd let me before she pulled away.

"Go."

I went and was outside on the porch and walking down the steps when her scream had me turning around.

"The bug!" She squealed.

I stifled a chuckle and shuffled back through the window.

She was pointing at the wall above my head.

Once through the window, I turned and saw the 'roach' she was talking about.

It wasn't a roach. It was a water bug.

A massive one at that.

"Give me that," I pointed at the rolled up wrapping paper she had standing in a corner of her room.

She hustled to it as much as an eight-month pregnant woman could, and tossed it to me.

I caught it one handed and immediately brought it down on top of the bug.

A resounding 'crunch' had me wincing.

Kitt made a gagging sound as I pulled the paper tube away, and then ran into the bathroom, coming out moments later with a wet wad of toilet paper in her hands.

"Here," she thrust the wet mass at me.

I rolled my eyes and handed her the tube, which she took with the utmost reluctance.

I heard tearing of the paper as I wiped the wall clean of bug guts.

"Here."

She took it and the wadded up paper and went to the bathroom.

While she was in there, I took my leave, knowing she'd want me to.

At least I thought.

I'd gotten nearly to my bike when she appeared at the window.

"Apple!" She cried, not seeing me in the dark where I'd parked.

I turned and studied her for a long moment, taking in the stricken look on her face that showed she wasn't happy with me leaving without her knowing.

"What?" I asked, coming forward out of the shadows.

Relief washed over her face once she saw me standing there.

"Come back tomorrow for dinner," she ordered.

I nodded.

"I can do that," I told her.

"And don't be late," she said.

I smiled.

"I won't," I promised.

"And wipe that look off your face. You didn't win," she ordered with a smile in her voice.

I rearranged my face so my smile didn't give away my excitement.

"Yes, Ma'am."

CHAPTER 13

Life is too short for boring socks.
-Kitt to Ridley

Kitt

I smiled as I finished making tacos.

Looking at my watch, I decided to chance the shower so I could smell good for Apple.

That and I had things that needed shaving.

I hadn't shaved the upper half of my thighs for about a month now, since I could no longer see them.

Not seeing the hair, and not having a man, definitely kept me from caring.

Not to mention I'd been a bit depressed over the last seven months.

It'd gotten so bad that some days I didn't want to get out of bed.

That was the good thing about having my brother, though. Not to mention those stolen moments with Apple when he went to my doctor's appointments with me.

Those two hours would be the best two hours of my entire week, and I'd spend the rest of my days counting down the minutes until the next doctor's appointment.

I'd also gotten on disability.

The impending doom of having a seizure at any time, and in any place, had made it almost impossible to hold down a job.

My doctor had signed the papers I needed to file for disability, which then had fed my hermit status.

I wasn't sure I'd gone out of the house for anything but doctor's appointments and my weekly grocery runs for well over six months.

I also didn't want to make it harder on the people I counted on. If it made it easier to stay at home, then I'd do it.

I'd just slipped my shirt off over my clothes and hung the t-shirt over the camera I now knew was in my bathroom when I got the expected phone call.

Sighing, I answered with a barely disguisable, angry, "Hello?"

"Hi, Kitt. It's Jake," the jovial man on the other end of the line said.

"Hi," I said. "I'm taking a shower."

"Yes, ma'am. I'm just instructed to call just in case. How are you doing today?" Jake spoke.

I gritted my teeth and barely contained the urge to hiss at him.

"I'm doing fine, thank you," I said stiffly. "Is there anything else?"

"Sure, now that you mention it. Some man came through your

window last night. I reported it to the account holder, and he said it was fine. Is that fine?" He chirped jovially.

I shivered.

Jake gave me the freakin' creeps.

And I hated that he watched me twenty-four hours a day.

I hated even more that Ridley gave him permission to.

When I'd asked Ridley to see about getting a new reviewer, he'd looked at me like I'd grown a second head.

"They have multiple people watching the feed every week. Which man is it that you don't like?" he asked.

"The one that calls here every time I cover my bathroom monitor," I replied.

He looked at me.

"You realize, right, that they're professionals?" He'd asked. "That they are supposed to call to make sure you're okay?"

After that I'd just ignored Jake and the uncomfortableness I felt each and every time I knew he was on the clock.

"Thank you, Jake. Have a nice night," I hung up.

Ignoring the way my skin crawled at the thought of that man watching my every move, I got into the shower and sighed when the scalding water touched my skin.

I loved hot showers. The hotter the better in my opinion.

The water sluiced down over my body, and I giggled happily when the baby started to move.

She loved the water, too.

That, and she liked that I wasn't hunched in a sitting position, which allowed her to move freely without any constraints.

I pushed in on my belly and smiled when she pushed out moments later.

"You're going to be so much fun," I whispered to her.

"Who are you talking to?" Apple asked from the other side of the door.

I squealed in surprise.

"Jesus, Apple!" I exclaimed. "You scared the dickens out of me!"

His dark eyes peered at me through the clear glass.

"Did you just say 'dickens'?" He teased.

I splashed water at him.

"What are you doing in here?" I narrowed my eyes. "You're still in the dog house."

He smiled then.

"Yeah, I guessed that. But Ridley got a call from the surveillance people saying that you had a camera out in the bathroom and I just wanted to come check on you…just in case," he said, his eyes watching the water as it slid down my body.

I rolled my eyes.

"Fucking Jake," I growled.

"What?" He rumbled, his eyes snapping back up to mine.

"I said I'm fine. Now, why don't you go eat while I finish my shower?" I asked.

"But I want to wait for you," he grumbled.

"Okay," I conceded. "But you can still get out."

His eyes took one last long look at my body, and then he disappeared just as silently as he'd arrived.

My body shivered at that long look.

I was happy that he still found me attractive. Especially if that hard-on in his pants indicated anything.

Rubbing my hands lovingly over my belly, I finished with my shower, shaved my insanely long leg hair, and walked out into my room without thinking about the camera.

Mainly because, once my feet hit the soft rug outside of the shower, I saw that Apple had left the door to my bedroom open.

I also saw that his long legs were stretched out on my bed; he was asleep.

I'd been fifteen minutes longer, at most, and I'd obviously given him too much time alone without proper stimulation to keep him awake.

I wrapped the towel around myself and made my way to the bed, letting my gaze linger on his tired face.

He was probably beyond exhausted due to how much he did.

On top of him working, I saw him nearly every night until I went to bed. Once my light flipped out, I'd hear his bike start up and head home.

Most nights.

Other nights, I would watch him watch me through the open window.

I still wasn't sure why he'd gotten into the habit of watching me.

Or why he wouldn't just come inside instead of staying outside.

But I guess that was answered last night, wasn't it?

I wanted to yell at him. Scream my indignation.

How could he keep us apart for this long over a look he thought I'd given him?

Seriously? Who did that?

But as I saw the bags under his eyes, I realized then that his wounds weren't superficial. They were deep, and they wanted to hold on and dig deeper.

And he'd been letting them fester.

He'd been letting them get so rotted and infected that he didn't even realize how bad they were because he couldn't feel them.

All he knew was that he was hurting. He just didn't know how badly.

"How long are you going to stare at me with your towel wrapped precariously around yourself?" Apple asked with a rumble, his voice thick with sleep.

I smiled at him and walked to the dresser that was holding my underthings.

I thought about going into the bathroom to get dressed, but I chose to test him.

If this wasn't real…he'd leave. The moment my towel dropped to the ground, he'd be gone, and I'd know if he was serious about staying with me or not. About giving us a chance.

You just can't hide emotions like that.

And the moment I dropped my towel, my back to Apple, I heard his swift intake of breath saw into his lungs.

"Ah, God," Apple groaned. "You're trying to kill me. I know it."

I laughed at him, tossing him a look over my shoulder that clearly said 'yes.'

"I knew it," he crowed. "That look you just threw at me was confirmation enough."

I grinned and bent over, giving him a clear view as I lifted one leg to put my panties on.

The sexiness fell out of it, though, when I had to catch and steady myself on the dresser.

My belly really didn't offer me very much stability lately, and now that I was so far along, it was getting worse.

"I usually have to sit down to do this," I told him when he started to laugh.

Apple groaned as he got up, and I was attempting a second try at putting my foot into the hole on my panties when he was there.

He dropped down to one knee and my hand automatically went to his shoulder as he helped me get my panties on.

Pulling them up slowly, he leaned forward and placed a kiss on my still growing belly.

"You're the most beautiful woman I've ever seen," he whispered.

My eyes closed in pleasure as he let his hands slip from the waistband of my underwear to move up to my belly where he cupped it as best as he could with both hands.

"I've been dying to do this," he pressed another kiss just under my belly button.

And our daughter, the playful little thing that she was, immediately kicked out where he'd pressed his lips, and Apple's eyes lit with pleasure.

"I never thought to see your badass self on your knees for me," I whispered to him, letting my fingers play along the length of his beard.

It'd gotten longer over the last couple of months.

Where before it'd just barely been a slightly overgrown beard, probably only days past needing trimmed, now it was blatantly grown out…and I fucking loved it.

I wanted to feel that beard on my skin as he kissed every single inch of my body.

"Your eyes are on fire," he looked up at me. "What are you thinking?"

I turned my face down to study his eyes, and I liked how he couldn't stop his gaze from falling down to my unbound breasts before he tried to look me into the eyes again.

I had mercy on him and reached for a sports bra, one of the only things I found comfortable anymore, and pulled it on over my head.

"I think we need to get out of my room before this goes further than we should be going right now," I told him honestly.

He laughed and pressed his thumb in, getting another nudge from our daughter.

"Are you excited?" He asked my stomach.

I assumed he was asking me that and not the baby, because I was sure that the child we'd made together never wanted to leave. She loved being exactly where she was.

Especially seeing as she was still head up, and I wasn't dilated or effaced a single tiny bit.

According to my doctor, if she didn't turn, they wouldn't risk me trying a natural birth. He'd go straight to a C-section because he didn't want to cause me any undue stress and accidentally throw me into a seizure.

Which would be bad.

I wanted to be awake for the birth of my child. Not in the comatose state that I always ended up in after my seizures.

"What are you thinking about up there?" Apple interrupted my worries.

I looked down at him and lifted my hand to run over his head.

His hair had a crease in it from where his cowboy hat sat atop his head for the entire day.

He was also still in his uniform, meaning he'd come over here directly after getting off of work.

"I was thinking about my birthing options," I said honestly. "Yes, I'm excited, but I just hope it all goes according to plan, and I don't have to end up having a C-section."

His eyes shuttered as did his body as he stood.

Our baby had fallen asleep in the last couple of minutes of play, and I wanted to roll my eyes.

The kid did this every night. She slept for the hours before I went to bed, and then proceeded to keep me up for over five hours in the middle of the night while she rolled, kicked, and played.

Apple's hands came up to cup my face, and he leaned in to place a kiss on my lips, but my phone rang.

He ignored it in favor of kissing me, and I couldn't say I was upset about that.

His tongue pressed between my lips, curling up to tease the tip of my mine.

My hands tightened in his hair, which I hadn't let go when he stood, pulling him even closer into me.

His big body was bowed around mine, curling around my belly and pulling me as close as he could.

And when he finally let me go, my brain was fuzzy.

"Food," I whispered, moving away from him to gasp in a breath.

He smiled just as my phone started ringing again.

"Guess someone's looking for you," he murmured.

I shrugged.

"Ridley knows you're here," I shrugged. "He wouldn't bother to call to check on me."

Apple grinned as he let go of me only long enough to grab my phone off the dresser that I'd brought with me from the bathroom, and answer it without looking at the caller ID.

I let go of him as I grabbed a t-shirt from the dresser drawer, smiling when I found my favorite on top.

I slipped it on over my head and turned just in time to see Apple's eyes narrow.

"Who is this?" Apple asked.

His brows furrowed and mine rose in question.

"Who is it?" I asked him, bending down to the bottom drawer and grabbing a pair of shorts.

These were ones I hadn't worn in a while, but with everything else dirty, I either had those or nothing.

So I chose those while watching his face to gauge his mood.

Which wasn't good.

"I can assure you that she's fine. If you're unsure, feel free to call the cops and the owner of the contract," Apple barked into the phone.

My brows crawled up into my hairline as I sat on the bed and pulled my shorts on.

I then had to laugh when I saw how tight they were.

They were also digging uncomfortable into my belly, so I rolled them down until they came to a rest underneath it.

Apple growled and hung up, turning to survey the camera that was in the corner of my room.

"Let me guess," I said, standing up. "It was Jake?"

He looked over at me and nodded.

"How'd you know?"

"Because Jake's a douche, and he gives me the creeps. He calls me each and every time I go into the bathroom and cover up the feed," I lifted my lip in a silent snarl.

His brows furrowed.

"There's one in the bathroom?" He looked ill.

I nodded and took his hand as I passed, taking him to the one in the bathroom and pointing to my shirt over it.

"Sometimes your brother annoys the shit out of me," he said. "Why would he put one in the bathroom?"

"Because he's worried I might fall out and die," I repeated Ridley's exact words. "But there's no way, now that I know about them, that I can take a shower in the bathroom or use the restroom while that's on. The majority of the time it stays covered until Ridley comes home and takes it down."

"Well, if someone's here with you, there's no reason for you to have it up. Tell him that next time," Apple replied angrily.

I smiled, knowing that I, at least, had Apple on my side.

"Let's go get dinner before I decide to ride to wherever that motherfucker is and fuck his face up," Apple growled, walking up to me and taking my hand.

I snorted.

"You should be careful what you say or he'll hear you and complain to Ridley," I said soothingly.

"Fuck them both."

With that eloquent statement, Apple left the room, leaving me smiling at his back as he went.

***

Dinner and the rest of the night had been magical, but the moment Ridley arrived home at ten, I'd sent Apple home.

Why?

Because he was falling asleep on his feet.

He hadn't been happy to be sent away, but the promise of seeing him in the morning before he went to work had given him enough incentive to leave even when he didn't want to go.

And now here I was, three oh three in the morning, and I was wide awake because his child liked to play.

I'd been awake for going on an hour when I decided that a visit to Apple was in order.

Certainly if I had to be up because of his child, so did he.

Right?

I knew it totally contradicted the entire reason I'd sent him home, but I wasn't thinking clearly any more. I was running on just as much, if not less, sleep than him.

I decided I *was* right after another twenty minutes of second guessing myself.

Getting up, I walked to my closet door and grabbed the first pair of shoes I could find, which happened to be my boots.

Then I went to the bathroom and gathered up the shorts I'd slipped on after my shower.

Once I'd slipped both my shorts and boots on, I grabbed my sweatshirt off the back of my chair and opened my window.

Luckily, I'd covered my camera before I'd gone to bed, or Ridley would be receiving a call right about now telling him I was trying to sneak out.

Why he'd get one, I didn't know. I was a grown ass adult, but since I knew Jake was on duty, I knew he'd think it necessary to call Ridley 'in case I hurt myself'.

Or whatever shit he'd come up with for calling.

Ridley was absolutely crazy if he didn't see that something was wrong with that weird man who watched my every move.

Apple realized it with one single phone call.

Ridley had dozens, and he still didn't see the big deal.

I contemplated this for the entirety of my walk, and had just come to the decision that I'd be bringing this up with Ridley tomorrow when I arrived to Apple's driveway.

I smiled when I wasn't met with just one, but three of Apple's dogs.

I wasn't actually sure the exact number he had, but I was sure there were more than just the three.

"Hello," I sang to the dogs.

Their tails swished in the dirt, and I touched each of their heads once as I walked past.

They didn't move from their spot, and I was tempted to walk around them to see if I could get them to move.

But my eyes were already heavy, and my ankles were hurting from the walk.

Not to mention my back, which always seemed to hurt lately, was killing me.

And then there was my pubic bone.

That one felt like it was cracking each time I took a step.

I'd asked my doctor, on one of my many visits, if it was normal for a pubic bone to feel like it was about to crack in half, and he'd said it was more than normal. That it was the ligaments that were stretching and preparing for birth that were the cause.

Knowing that it was normal didn't make it better, though.

I still hurt like a motherfucker each time I took a step. Or moved wrong. Or rolled over in bed. Or painted my toes.

Okay, it hurt all the fucking time.

I didn't think there was a time it didn't hurt, unless I was sleeping and able to ignore it.

Except I wasn't sleeping all that much, now was I?

"Goodnight, doggies," I called as I walked past them and down the driveway.

I went straight to the barn, closing the door behind me as I went inside.

My eyes went straight up the stairs to find the huge barn doors up top closed as well, which meant that Apple was likely in there with the air conditioner on.

He'd said he rarely closed them unless the air was on, and even though it was only February, it'd been in the mid-eighties all week.

It cooled down at night, but the big barn was fast to heat up, and slow to cool down, according to one of our few conversations.

So I climbed the stairs, wincing with each step.

Once I reached the barn doors, I slid one door softly open just far enough that I could squeeze inside, and closed it just as soundlessly behind myself.

Then I looked to the bed where Apple was laying, and I strongly urged myself not to do it.

I really shouldn't have.

I swear to God, I was telling myself not to, but the way he was sleeping so peacefully with his hands tucked under his face like a fucking angel had my eyes narrowing.

"Apple!" I bellowed.

He sat up in the bed like he'd been cattle prodded, his eyes crazy, as he looked around the room sightlessly.

It was then I saw the gun in his hand.

I never said I made smart decisions.

Sometimes they were terrible decisions, in fact.

Like starting paralegal school. Or working at a gas station graveyard shift. Or having unprotected sex because I thought my medication rendered me infertile.

Yes, I made terrible decisions, and seeing Apple with a gun in his hand pointed at the roof had my eyes widening.

"Shit," I apologized. "I'm sorry."

His eyes finally turned to me, and he narrowed them dangerously low.

"What. The. Fuck," he said through clenched teeth. "I could have shot you."

"Well, aren't you glad I'm over here waking you up rather than standing over you?" I asked, hoping playing light of the situation would bring the tension level in the room down minutely.

It didn't.

In fact, he got angrier.

"Next time, call," he said through a growl.

I narrowed my eyes, then turned around and threw the barn doors open.

"Maybe next time I won't come at all," I threw over my shoulder as I started to stomp down the stairs.

It hurt like a bitch to do, too. But I did it.

I made it all the way to the bottom and about five steps into the hayloft before I felt him behind me.

I would've ran if I wasn't humongous elephant pregnant, but I did have some sense, after all.

So I continued my pace towards the set of barn doors that would lead outside, trying to ignore the impending doom I could feel baring down on me.

And bare down it did.

He had his hand around my waist, pulling me back against his chest - his naked chest, might I add - in the next second.

He stopped me with another hand in my hair.

"How about you check the attitude and tell me what was so important that you just scared the shit out of me and nearly got shot for?" He whispered gratingly against my ear.

His beard tickled my neck, and his words, although threatening, made my seriously in need of a fucking vagina, clench with need.

Shivers raced down my spine at the deadly quiet of his tone. The seriousness of it.

I was horny.

I was emotional.

I was in need of a good fucking.

That was the stitch.

I needed it, and he needed to give it to me.

But I didn't want nice and sweet Apple.

I found that I wanted a rough and little bit angry Apple.

The one I'd woken up and scared ten years off his life.

"Why the fuck do you care?" I asked. "I just wanted to see if you were where you said you were going to be."

His body, which had been loosening, tightened back up again.

"What did you say?" He asked carefully.

I turned, and with him not letting go of my hair, it made his grip seem tighter even though he hadn't moved so much as an inch.

My belly pushed him even further away, but he didn't seem to notice as he glared into my eyes.

The only thing that was lighting the dark room around us was a single harsh bulb high above our heads, casting an eerie yellow glow in about a five-foot radius all around us.

The shadows on Apple's face made him appear more sinister, and even though I was loathe to admit it, he looked even hotter.

And the anger I could see in his eyes, as well as the stiff way he held his body, was clearly not conveying the correct information.

At least not to me.

"You heard me," I said, poking him with a stiffened finger in the chest.

His bare chest.

And as I looked down, his even barer lower half.

I say barer because his chest had a smattering of chest hair that I'd never actually seen before.

We'd had sex all of two times together, and I'd yet to see him without his shirt on.

I could see scars.

In fact, my finger was directly in the middle of one scar that started at his collarbone and curled around his pectoral muscle, making a divot where it trailed through.

I could also see something wrong with his right shoulder, but the second my eyes lit on the mangled flesh, his hand that'd been around my body was now fastened to my chin. Holding my face in place so I couldn't let my eyes drift beyond where he wanted me to look.

"Don't look at me," he ordered.

I laughed in his face.

"I can look at you if I want to look at you. You're mine, aren't you?" I challenged him. "Or was what you said two days ago a lie? Maybe you don't really want me like you say you want me."

His eyes narrowed, and a glow seemed to light from somewhere deep within him.

His hand that'd been in my hair pulled me impossibly closer, and the one that was on my chin let go of me and took up a place in my hair as well.

"How about you drop to your knees and see how much I don't want you?" He suggested vulgarly. "Take my hard cock in your mouth and *see*."

I think he thought that maybe by being crude like that, I'd leave him alone long enough for him to regain control.

Control that he so desperately needed.

He was obviously worried that he'd scare me away if he showed me this side of him, and I just knew that I had to break through the wall.

I had to let him know that I could handle all of him.

The scars. The anger. The self-loathing.

I had to prove to him that I could handle all that he had to give, even if what he had to give wasn't all that great, before he'd give himself over fully to me.

Although this wasn't what I'd come here to accomplish, it seemed like as good of a time as any to get this over with.

I'd been holding my anger in for months.

I was so pissed off, and still was, that he'd dropped me as if I was nothing to him, all because of some look I gave him and he misread.

To be honest, I had a lot of pent up anger that I would love to unleash on him.

Starting now.

"How about I get on my knees so you can treat me like a whore. A faceless nobody that can't see your body. Doesn't know anything about you," I said snidely. "Is that what you want me to be? Someone who looks pretty on your arm, who has your kid, but doesn't ask you for anything else? Maybe someone who's not fucked up like I am?"

His eyes narrowed. "I don't want anybody else."

"Well, you could've fooled me, *Apple*," I hissed, poking his left pec with my right pointer finger as I rose up on my toes to get my face into his. "Most people that want someone go after them. What have you done?"

I really didn't know why I was antagonizing him the way I was.

Clearly I'd lost my mind, as well as the filter on my mouth. Otherwise, I would've seen the state I was working him into.

But I didn't.

I just kept going. And going. And going.

Until suddenly, he just snapped.

One second I was poking him in the chest, and the next I was on my knees while he grabbed a hold of his cock.

My knees were on the cool wood floor of the barn, and I was extremely turned on.

But I couldn't let him handle me like this. I was pregnant after all. Weren't you supposed to act a certain way when you were pregnant?

I opened my mouth to protest, but before I could get a single word out, my mouth was filled with him.

"Obviously," he said through clenched teeth. "You need something constructive to do with that mouth."

I moaned around his cock, causing him to hiss in a breath of air.

"Now you'll listen to me," he said. "Suck it. Move your mouth on my cock." He made a sound of approval. "That's it. Use your hand. Good girl."

I did as instructed, moving my mouth up and down his shaft while I copied the rhythm I'd set with my hand.

I pulled back and let my tongue circle the tip of his penis, tasting a drop of pre-come that leaked out of his cock.

"Are you listening?" He growled. "Give me your eyes and let me know you hear me."

I looked up at him, sucking the tip of his throbbing cock back into my mouth, and gave him my eyes.

"I fucking love you. I've loved you since you said you liked my goats," he said.

I blinked, backing off slightly.

"No, don't stop," he ordered, tightening his hold in my hair and roughly shoving himself further into my mouth.

I kept going, but my heart, not to mention my mouth, was full to bursting.

All I wanted to do was to stand up and impale myself on his cock.

But I was logical.

I was thirty-two weeks pregnant, and there was no way I could climb him like a proverbial tree.

That, and I wanted to hear what else the man had to say.

And I was glad I kept going, licking, sucking, and teasing.

Because he gave me what I wanted.

"I suffer from depression," he said through a pant. "And I wake up sometimes and my head's not in a good place. But all I have to do is think of you and our baby we made, and it makes everything okay. Not good, but okay. The only thing—the only thing, Kitt—that makes it better is when you're with me. Every day. I'm tired. I'm just so goddamned tired of fighting everything, baby."

His eyes stayed on mine, and despite his telling me not to stop, I did anyway.

I let his cock slip from my mouth with a nice long lick down the length of his shaft, and then got up.

He didn't protest this time.

His hands did stay in my hair, however.

"I know we haven't spent much time together," I said to him, moving as close as his cock and my belly would allow. "But not a day has gone by, since I met you, that I haven't thought about you. In fact, it would be safe to say not a single day has gone by where I haven't thought about you several times. I can't even tell you how many times I've wished you were there holding me at night. I'm damn tired, too, of fighting what I feel for you, and I honestly don't want to do it anymore. I'm fucked up. Beyond fucked up. You're fucked up. Apple, why can't we just be fucked up together?"

"I'm possessive," he warned, pulling my face closer to his.

I laughed.

"So?" I challenged.

"I have to take medication," he informed me.

I smiled, grabbing a hold of his cock and pumping it softly.

It was still hard enough to pound nails. Sleek, smooth skin wrapped around a rock hard shaft. So hard, in fact, that he could probably fuck me for hours without slowing.

"I don't know if you're aware, but I take medication, too," I told him.

He pressed a wet kiss against my lips, trailing his tongue along the seam of my lips.

"I have nightmares."

He was letting it all hang out.

Good, me too.

"I don't sleep," I told him.

A grin kicked up the corner of his mouth.

"I like my job, and I'm gone a lot during hunting season," he informed me.

I laughed against his lips.

"Honey, this is the South. It wouldn't be right if I had a man and didn't lose him during hunting season," I informed him. "In fact, I think it's against our religion or something if you don't hunt."

"I'm a cover hog," he kept it up. "And I don't like people eating my food."

"Is that right?" I asked, squeezing his length.

His eyes brightened.

"Yeah. That's right," he murmured. "Can't stand it when people eat my food. Or when I have to eat last. Or when I'm forced to clean up other people's food."

"So it's something about food that has your feathers ruffled?" I confirmed.

He shrugged.

"Don't know. Don't care. I'm just giving you fair warning not to fuck with my food," he informed me.

I wanted to laugh, but I didn't dare.

"Anything else?" I challenged.

He started backing up, and seeing as my hand was still wrapped around his cock, I chose to follow.

He backed up until he hit the wall, and there he flipped on the light switches that lit up the barn, as well as the room upstairs.

"Follow me," he ordered, pulling my hand free of his cock and turning to go upstairs once again.

I watched him walk away, my eyes first on the way that his cock bounced as he walked.

Then on the way his ass flexed as he took the stairs.

Then I got sidetracked as I watched his balls sway slightly with his movements each time he lifted a leg up to the next step.

Then he stopped, one foot on the step above him, and he looked over his shoulder at me.

"Come," he ordered.

Oh, I was going to.

Guaranteed.

The moment I finally made it up the stairs, my pubic bone still killing me, I stopped when I found Apple sitting on the bed with his back to me.

"It's bad," he rumbled. "And it hurts. It never stops hurting. It's a constant reminder of what I failed to do."

I blinked as tears started to form in my eyes.

Walking forward, I placed my hand on his unmarred shoulder, causing him to flinch at my touch.

Once he regained control, I let my hand trail along his back.

My belly pressed up against his spine, and our little girl rolled and flipped at the confined movement, causing Apple to relax even more.

I let my fingers run along the scars that covered his left shoulder.

It looked like something had come up and taken a huge bite out of the back of him.

Although he was still muscular, his shoulder looked badly scarred and misshapen.

You'd never be able to tell, though, from the front.

He was still just as defined, muscularly, everywhere but there.

In fact, if you weren't actively looking for the mottled skin, it was likely no one would be able to see it at all.

Especially with the clothes he wore.

It was only now, with his shirt off and back exposed, that I could see it. I could see the real damage that'd almost taken his life.

"You're lucky," I whispered.

"I'm not lucky," he said harshly. "This is sometimes worse than losing a limb. There are days that I want to hack off my arm because the pain gets so bad."

I let my belly press even further into his back as I wrapped my hands around his neck, pressing my lips against his shoulder in a gentle kiss.

"You're here," I whispered. "We have a baby on the way. I count that as lucky in my book."

His head dropped into his hands, and I leaned backward and shucked the sweatshirt from my body.

The next thing to go was the t-shirt, then the shorts and panties.

I kicked the boots off last, and then walked around the bed where he was sitting and stopped when my breasts met his head.

My belly was poking against his chin, but he didn't seem to mind.

He lifted his hands to my stomach, and his head rested against my bare breasts, as he breathed in swiftly.

My hands headed to his hair, where I worked my fingers gently through the long strands.

The movement let my breasts play against his beard, and I had to actively stop myself from moving them on purpose.

His hands skimmed away from my belly where they curved down and around to my ass.

He then cupped it and spread my ass cheeks apart, letting my overheated core become exposed to the cool air.

Then his hands sank in further until both sets of fingers were in between my lips.

His head came up and, instinctively, I placed one breast against his mouth.

He sucked it in between his lips, letting his tongue play along the turgid tip.

"Ah, God," I whispered, my body jerking in surprise.

My breasts were beyond sensitive before, but now they felt like they were on steroids with the way I was responding to his ministrations.

"I want to fuck you," he whispered. "I want to bend you over that dresser, then shove my cock so far into your pussy that you feel it in your throat."

I moaned and pulled away from him.

My breast left his mouth with a small sucking pop, and I smiled.

His hands tightened on me, and I had to stifle a moan as two fingers slipped into my tight heat.

"Let go," I urged him gently.

He did, letting his hands slip from the folds of my sex.

I watched in stunned silence as he brought his fingers up to his mouth and licked them clean of my juices, like one would do after they've finished eating a delicious meal.

Moaning in the back of my throat, I moved so that my back was against him, walking to the dresser where I braced my elbows on the edge of the wood and aimed my ass backwards toward him.

"Come fuck me then," I urged.

His eyes flared and he stood up and started towards me.

I watched him move, turning to face forward, delighting in the fact that I could see him in the mirror.

His eyes were hard and demanding as he prowled towards me.

His cock was bobbing, and his balls were swinging.

I licked my lips and popped my ass out even further.

The movement placed my breasts against the cool, rough wood.

But I didn't care.

I was too focused on watching him fist his cock, working it in three rough pulls, causing a small drop of white fluid to leak out the end to bead up on his tip.

My mouth watered as I watched him wipe it off with a finger, then bring that same finger to my lips.

I licked the drop of pre-come off his finger, then sucked the entire thing into my mouth.

"Jesus Christ," he hissed, his cock jerking against my ass.

He pulled his finger roughly away from me, taking a hold of my ass with both hands.

Then without any aid at all, he guided his cock to my pussy and slowly sank inside.

He filled me up so completely that I wanted to scream.

"I want to hear you," he ordered. "Let me know just how much you like having my cock filling you up."

I moaned and dropped my head, unable to watch him anymore.

I was so close to coming that it wasn't funny, but he didn't like not having my eyes.

Which was more than evident when he tugged on my hair and said, "Eyes."

I gave him my eyes, my breath coming out in pants.

He moved his cock out of my pussy and then thrust back inside.

The move was so slick that I knew he had to be completely saturated with my juices.

I'd found, over many nights of masturbation, that I somehow became wetter since I'd become pregnant.

The moment my fingers touched my clit, I was instantly ready.

But this, with Apple, was different.

I was almost embarrassed by the amount of fluid that was coming from my body.

But he fucking loved it, seeing as he told me in the next instant.

"I love how your pussy sounds taking my cock," he growled, his jaw going hard as his eyes went down to where we were connected.

I longed to see the sight, but seeing the rapture that flashed over Apple's face was definitely just as good.

"I wish I could have my mouth on you and cock in you at the same time," he growled. "Taste you while I felt you around me all at once."

I moaned, my eyes going hooded, as I listened to him talk dirty to me.

Paired with the way he was fucking me, I was fighting with everything I had not to come.

"Don't hold back," he said, his eyes now on me.

I shook my head.

"I'm so close," I gasped.

"Then come. Give me you."

I gave him me.

I came, hard.

So hard that my eyes automatically closed to keep them from falling out of my head from the pressure that built up in my body.

My pussy clamped down on him, and he ramped up the speed.

His thighs hitting the backs of mine so hard that loud smacking sounds filled the room along with the sounds of my wet sex taking his big, hard cock.

"Goddamn," he growled. "Goddammit you feel so good. Like a fucking dream."

My mouth dropped open as a scream poured out of my mouth.

His hand in my hair and on my ass clenched, and his face closed down.

Everything tightened. His jaw. His lips. His chest and abs.

His eyes narrowed.

Then he was filling me up, giving me everything that was him.

It was agony and pure bliss at the same time.

Another orgasm blindsided me, taking me back under with him.

Stars exploded behind my closed eyelids, and the scream from before had taken all my oxygen with it, meaning when that first gasp of air entering my lungs was pure pleasure added on top of my already exploding orgasm.

My legs collapsed, and Apple's arm around my hips were the only things stopping me from hitting the floor.

I opened my eyes and watched him watch me.

His eyes taking in everything.

My nipples that were red and aggravated from rubbing along the rough wood.

My cheeks were flushed from my orgasm.

Then there was my hair.

The ponytail it'd once been in was no more. It hung in a lopsided mess against the side of my head, stray strands of hair fell down, framing my face.

My lips were swollen.

"You're so goddamn beautiful," he rasped, his eyes looking straight into mine.

I felt a smile break out across my face.

"You're not so bad yourself."

CHAPTER 14

We go together like fuck and you.
-Kitt to Apple

Apple

"You're buying my lunch, aren't you?" Ridley asked.

I tossed a look at him over my shoulder.

"I don't remember saying that," I mumbled. "I'll let you eat lunch with me, though."

Ridley snorted and took a seat, Wolf on the other side of me.

"Saw the bust you got," Wolf muttered as he brought his glass of milk closer to him.

I turned my head to study him.

"How'd you hear that already?" I asked.

The bust had only happened this morning. Or what he was referring to as a bust.

It was more like I caught two trappers being dumbasses, trying to kill alligators without having the proper licensing.

"They had four dead gators in the back of their flat bottom. Shit like that seems to spread fast in a town like this," Ridley added his two cents.

"Fuck yeah," I sighed in exhaustion.

I'd stayed up late into the night talking to Kitt, and I'd had to be at work at six this morning.

Staying up late was not conducive with a job that required you to get there early and stay late.

"You should've heard this shit going over the police scanner," Wolf chuckled. "I couldn't tell whether you got a live alligator or not."

"Oh, one of them was alive," I mumbled. "Had to go fucking release it, too. Couldn't do it at the boat dock, meaning I had to take it, fucking alive, about ten miles downstream."

Wolf chuckled and I nodded to the waitress that brought me another drink.

"You coming to the party tonight?" Ridley asked, taking a bite of his pie that the waitress had set down in front of him when I'd gotten my refill.

"Have a fucking press conference this afternoon," I mumbled tiredly. "I'll see what it's looking like timewise once I'm done with it."

"Kitt's going," Ridley said experimentally.

I snorted.

"I know. It's a fucking baby shower for our kid," I shot back.

"Why wouldn't I know?"

He shrugged.

"I thought you were trying to keep it secret that you spent the night with her, that's all," he said lightly.

I turned only my head in his direction.

"How do you know that I was spending time with her?" I mumbled.

"Because I saw her sneak out of her room last night, then I followed her to your place," he said lightly.

I sighed.

"She thinks she covered the camera. She didn't find all the cameras, did she?" I said carefully.

He shook his head.

"Put two in there," he said.

"She's going to fucking kill you."

"She'll never figure it out," he shot back.

I rolled my eyes.

She would be finding out, especially after I told her

"Can you take Kitt to her doctor's appointment tomorrow?" I asked Ridley, getting off the subject of those cameras.

"No," he said. "I have to be in court at eleven, and I'm short two deputies."

I pinched the bridge of the nose.

As much as I hated to do it, I'd have to ask him to ask Capone.

"You'll have to ask Capone," I said stiffly.

Corey Capone was one of the deputies that worked with Ridley, and the man that'd been in the car the day I'd gone to see her at the hospital that first time.

Overall, I supposed he was a nice guy.

But I didn't need a nice guy around Kitt.

I already had my work cut out for me with her.

I'd done a lot of soul searching over these last few months.

I'd also spent quite a bit of time reflecting on my life, as well as seeing a man about my fucked up head.

And what I'd found, I didn't like.

"So you are coming?" Wolf asked.

I nodded. "I'm coming. Even if I fall asleep during it."

***

Five hours later, and one hour late, I parked my bike outside the clubhouse.

The bottom half of my clothes were wet, my balls were chafing against the inside of my wet underwear, and I was in a shit mood.

But I was here.

My feet were dragging, mostly because they were tired, but also quite possibly due to the fact that my boots were waterlogged.

"You're late," Peek stated the obvious, his accent thicker than usual.

I looked up and felt my neck pop.

My shoulder ached like a bitch, and I winced.

"I had a mishap," I admitted, gesturing to my wet clothes.

Peek snorted.

"You want to change your clothes?" He asked.

I nodded.

"Yeah," I rumbled. "I'm goin' around back."

Peek took a drag of his cigarette and nodded, watching me as I walked around the side of the house.

Once I hit the back deck steps, I took them one at a time.

My eyes stayed on the wooden beam beneath my feet and not where I was going, which was why I didn't see her until I was less than a few inches from her.

"Hey, Mary," I said, shifting so I could move around her.

Mary's hand touched my cheek.

"You look tired," she said in that sultry tone she liked to use on any man she thought she could get something from.

I jerked my face out of her hand and pushed around her, causing her to move or fall.

She moved.

"What's gotten into you, darlin'?" She asked.

I ignored her and headed to the backdoor, wincing when the sound of the ladies laughing pierced through my frontal lobe and lodged somewhere in my brainstem.

This headache, paired with the fact that I had less than two hours of sleep, combined with the fact that I now had to go to a party with a bunch of giggling women put me in one hell of a bad mood.

I stomped through the kitchen and went straight through to the back hallway, not even stopping to say hi to anyone, let alone Kitt.

That was incredibly rude of me, but I thought if I stopped before I changed, I might very well collapse due to sensory overload.

Finding the door to the spare room I'd been allowed to use occasionally when I first started prospecting, I froze solid when I saw what was on the bed.

"Surprise," Kitt said quietly from directly behind me.

I didn't turn around.

I couldn't.

Not with the Uncertain Saints cut that was laying on my bed like some priceless artifact.

I rubbed my fingers along the name on the breast.

CORE.

It was stitched in blood red with the word 'member' directly beneath it.

"Holy fucking shit," I breathed softly.

"This is a double party," Kitt said at my back. "You patching in, and a shower for our baby all rolled into one."

I closed my eyes and fisted the smooth leather, bringing it up to my face and inhaling the strong scent.

"I'm proud of you," she continued, sewing my ripped up heart back together, one word at a time. "And why are your pants wet?"

I laughed and turned, surveying her.

My head which, might I add, was still pounding like a bitch, kicked once at the sight of her before me.

"You look beautiful," I whispered roughly.

She grinned and turned around.

"I'm just glad I was able to wear it. I bought it at the end of summer when they put all the winter stuff out. I wasn't sure if I'd ever get to wear it before the baby came," she twirled.

I admired the black and white chevron maxi dress that trailed all the way down to her bare feet, and grinned.

"You're not wearing your boots," I noticed.

She lifted up her foot to rest on the chair beside her and I winced.

"That's not normal," I told her.

She looked down at her swollen foot.

"According to my doctor, it's completely normal. I was told to put my feet up, but I haven't gotten the chance yet. I wanted this day to be perfect for you, too," she admitted.

I leaned forward and captured her hand, pulling her to me gently.

She moved her foot back to the floor and came willingly, right into my open arms.

A soft, hesitant knock sounded at the door, and both of us turned in time to see Mary peek through.

Completely nude.

"What. The. Fuck," I barked, startling her.

She looked freaked as her gaze bounced from me to Kitt and back.

"I'm sorry!" She squeaked, backing out of the door just as fast as she came.

"Who was that?" Kitt asked quizzically.

She didn't sound jealous. Just curious.

And that made me even more happy that she was trusting me.

Had the positions been reversed, I definitely wouldn't have handled it was well as she had.

"That's Mary," I said.

"Ahhh," she pursed her lips. "That's the girl that keeps trying to get Ridley to let her come home with him."

I nodded.

"She has no loyalty. Anyone that'll look at her and tell her she's pretty is good enough for her," I remembered the first and only time I'd slept with her.

And the thoughts must've shown on my face, because Kitt's eyes narrowed dangerously at me.

"What was that?" She stiffened, poking me in the chest just like she'd done the night before.

I caught her hand before that damn fingernail could poke me again, and I pulled her into me.

"Ewww," she winced, pushing away from me. "You smell like a

wet fish."

I chuckled against her hair.

"Kiss me," I ordered.

She shook her head quickly, pressing at my chest and pushing away so there would be a gap between her dry clothes and my wet ones.

I tossed my new cut onto the bed where it'd been earlier, and put two hands into the fight she wasn't going to be winning.

Something which she realized not twenty seconds later when she wasn't able to push more than an inch away from me.

Sighing in annoyance, she offered her lips up to me.

"You slept with her, didn't you?" She waited.

I nodded.

"Once," I informed her. "And I was drunk."

She sighed.

"It's nice to know that, at least, your sober self has a little bit of common sense," she teased.

I started unbuttoning my uniform shirt, a task which she promptly took over when she realized how slow I was at it.

"You don't have anything clean you could've changed into?" She wondered, her belly brushing my hand as she made quick work of my shirt.

I moved to allow the wet fabric to fall stiffly to the ground, and then started in on my pants.

"Where's your gun?" She asked when she saw my empty holster.

"It's at the bottom of Caddo Lake."

Her mouth dropped open.

"How did that happen?" She gasped.

"Fucking boneheaded teenager thought it'd be fun to do donuts in the stumps right outside of the state park," I muttered. "And when I went to get him into my boat, the dumbass pulled me in with him," I growled.

"And your gun?" She asked.

"Gone somewhere in the shuffle," I sighed. "Looked for it for about two hours before I decided to call it a day."

She blinked.

"That's kind of crappy," she confessed. "And this?"

She pointed to an angry red line that ran down the length of my forearm.

Luckily, my shirt was made of sturdy material, otherwise I would've probably needed stitches.

"Barbed wire," I said. "Fell and it caught me all the way up the arm."

"Why'd you fall?" She continued curiously.

"Because someone thought it'd be awesome to put their trot line above water so they could see it," I explained. "Fucking ran across it and caught myself on the barbed wire fence."

"Sounds like you've had an eventful day," she surmised, helping me take my belt off.

I pulled my underwear and pants down once my belt and pants were unbuttoned, then sat naked onto the bed with everything bunched up around my ankles.

I was bent over, head down to see my shoes, when the door burst open and not just the men of the club, but the women that belonged to the men, started filing in.

"Seriously?" I asked them, looking from my bare dick, to them, and back.

"Shit. Sorry, man," Griffin apologized. "Lenore, stop looking!"

Lenore rolled her eyes and turned her back so she was facing Griffin's chest.

Annie, Mig's wife, and Tasha, Casten's wife, also turned to give me privacy.

"You couldn't have done this later, Core?" Ridley called teasingly. "My sister's been dying to open these presents since she got here over two hours ago."

I bent back over after rolling my eyes and made quick work of untying my boots.

"You got something else to change into beside your cut and your birthday suit?" Wolf asked, his eyes amused.

I nodded.

"Clothes and shit in the bag in the closet," I told him.

"Well, you can unpack now since you're officially a part of the Uncertain Saints MC. Welcome to the club," Peek offered gruffly.

And that was how I was officially brought into the club.

***

"Your head still hurt?" Kitt asked against my chest.

I shook my head, even though it was killing me.

"I'm…"

I froze when Kitt started to convulse in my arms.

Her body stiffened, and her eyes went utterly blank.

I was up and moving before she'd even been in the seizure for less than ten seconds.

"Ridley!" I yelled, bouncing to my feet and yanking the bottle of meds off Kitt's bedside table.

They were in every room in the house, and they were always accessible for this very reason.

"You got it?" Ridley asked from the other side.

I tried to hand it to him, but he shook his head.

"It's better when you do it. She doesn't get as embarrassed," he assured me.

Gritting my teeth, I removed the syringe, yanked off the cap, placed some lubricating jelly on the tip that Ridley offered to me, and bent over the still convulsing Kitt.

My heart was hammering just like it always did when I was put into this position.

Pushing her over to her side, I moved her leg up and then set the tip against her anus, inserted it, and then pushed the meds into her.

The next few minutes passed as Ridley and I waited for the meds to take effect, and a collective breath of relief burst free of our chests as the convulsions finally stopped.

"God, they're getting longer and longer," Ridley mumbled, rubbing his eyes tiredly. "You need me?"

I shook my head and watched him leave.

Once he was gone, I pulled Kitt's panties back into place, went to the bathroom and tossed the syringe into the trash, and then washed my hands.

All the while, I kept my eyes on Kitt to make sure she didn't start up again.

Luckily, she didn't, and I left the bathroom, immediately getting into bed beside her and pulling her into my chest.

The baby immediately let me know that she was okay by kicking me, and I felt my chest loosen all the way.

"God," I breathed. "Goddammit."

CHAPTER 15

Sex is like a gas station. Sometimes you get full service, others you have to ask for service. And sometimes you have to be happy with self-service.
-Fact of Life

Ridley

My scanner squawked and I debated turning it off.

I was on my lunch break.

Or what I called my lunch break. Others might call it breakfast, but I'd been at work for over thirty-six hours now, and I'd only caught about an hour of shut eye since I'd arrived at work yesterday morning.

But something told me to leave it on. A sixth sense that had me leaving it on, as I shoved yet another hot dog into my face.

"All units in the area please respond. There's a multi-vehicle wreck on Interstate Twenty about four miles outside of Jefferson," a dispatcher said. "Any and all available units needed."

I sighed.

"Shit," I grumbled, taking the last hot dog that was on my plate with me as I left.

The cute little waitress that'd done her best to get me to look at her, all the while as I sat there eating my lunch, waved at me as I left.

I nodded at her, not wanting to encourage her behavior.

Her father owned the one and only gas station/grocery store called 'The Mall' in fifteen square miles, and it was inevitable that I ended up there at least once a shift.

Hurrying to my car, I finished off my hot dog before I'd even pulled out of the parking lot.

Picking up my radio, I called in to the station.

"I'm responding to the call on the interstate," I told the secretary that was there to answer our calls. "I'll be out of district for at least a couple of hours."

That was only a guess, though.

It could only be minutes, but would likely be quite a bit more than that.

When an accident happened on the interstate, it was probable that it involved more than one car.

I had my EMT license and would be of *some* help, even if only a little bit.

But by the time I arrived at the scene, I knew I'd be way more than just a few hours.

I'd be lucky if it was just six.

Finding the scene commander, I walked up to him and introduced myself.

"I'm Deputy Ridley Walker with the Harrison County Sheriff's

Office. What do you need from me?" I asked.

As I introduced myself, my eyes slowly scanned the scene, taking in the complete and utter chaos.

That's when my eyes lit on the familiar black truck that I'd let Capone borrow that morning. In fact, I'd pretty much demanded it, seeing as Capone had been nice enough to take Kitt to her doctor's appointment in the first place.

There was no reason that the man should have to put all those miles on his truck.

My truck was distinctive.

It had a yellow 'baby on board' sign hanging in the back window, with a sticker that declared the driver of the vehicle as a 'State Trooper Association Member.'

My dad had been a state trooper, and ever since he'd died, we'd been donating to the State Trooper's Association.

My sister, Kitt, had demanded I put that on my truck, and I'd done it.

Why? Because I loved my sister.

Now, seeing that sticker, something raw started to roll through my belly.

I hit my knees beside the overturned truck before the Incident Commander could even tell me where to go.

The men that were already surrounding the car looked at me, startled at my abrupt arrival, when I landed, but turned back to their business as soon as they realized they weren't coming to harm, but I was there to help.

My heart sank when I heard the paramedic's first words.

"…man is dead. The woman isn't though. Has a large gash across her forehead. My guess she's eight or nine months pregnant, too."

"Eight," I said roughly. "She's eight."

The paramedic looked at me over his shoulder and nodded. "You know her?"

I nodded tightly.

"She's my sister."

My belly rolling, I pulled out my phone and called the one person that was always there for me no matter what.

"Boyo?" Peek's thickly accent voice called loudly into the phone. "You better make this good. I'm between my wife's thighs, about three seconds away from being in the promise land."

"My sister. She's hurt. Accident," I said gruffly. "You need to handle Apple."

CHAPTER 16

Things could be worse. How, you ask? Sex could be fattening.
-Text from Kitt to Apple

Apple

Seven hours prior

"If you know what's good for you, you'll be back at a normal time tonight," Kitt said to me, grabbing my hat that'd been on the foot of the bed and placing it on the top of my head with a small smile gracing her beautiful lips.

My eyes shifted from the buttons I was trying to fasten to her face.

"And why's that?" I asked, finishing the buttons and pulling her into my arms.

She came willingly, tipping my hat up with her finger before going up on her toes to give me a kiss.

"Because I have a special congratulatory dinner planned," she informed me. "And I've got plans to move your clothes from your house to mine."

I blinked, surprised.

"Yeah?" I asked. "How are you going to do that?"

She grinned.

"Your father has agreed to loan the use of his scooter," she giggled. "But I'm not getting much. Just enough to get you through the weekend."

"So you're going to hold me hostage for five days?" I asked. "What are you going to do once those days are up?"

She pouted slightly.

"Send you back to work, I suppose," she shrugged. "And not see you for days on end."

I bent down and placed a kiss on the tip of her nose.

"I stayed away and did overtime because I wanted to keep my mind occupied," I explained to her gently. "I won't have to do that anymore, unless I want to."

Her eyes flared with an inner light that I couldn't quite decipher before she was suddenly very naked.

Her shirt was ripped over her head and thrown to the floor before I even had a chance to protest.

"Work…" I said. "I have one more day of work. Then we can do as much fucking off as we want."

She giggled.

"Did I tell you how sexy you look in only your work shirt, boxers, and a cowboy hat?" She asked, circling her finger around the emblem on my work shirt.

"No," I snorted. "You didn't mention that before."

Personally, I thought I looked ridiculous, but there was a method to my madness.

Shirt on first, followed by underwear, pants, socks and then boots.

Since my shirt had to be tucked in, it seemed to easier to get that on first, and obviously Kitt approved of my methods.

I caught her hands when she started to go a little too far south, and she grinned.

"You're going to be on time, promise," she said, pulling her hands from mine and letting them trail down my sides. "You'll make this quick."

I groaned in defeat when she pressed her unbound breasts against my arm and dragged them along the coarse hair before walking to the bed and laying down.

The position made the t-shirt she was wearing slide up past her hips and expose her bared pussy to me.

"You're sure?" I asked, putting a knee on the bed between her splayed thighs.

Her eyes, already hooded, lowered further.

Then she widened her legs in invitation.

An invitation that I didn't ignore.

Crawling up between her legs, I stopped when my thighs touched hers.

"So are you ready for me?" I ran the backs of my fingers up her leg lightly.

Up and down I went as I watched small goosebumps break out over the sensitive skin.

She gasped slightly, her breath hitching in anticipation when my fingers ventured close to her pussy lips.

"I'm more than ready," she whispered. "I watched you shower and played with myself."

My eyebrows shot to the top of my head at her words.

"You're a dirty girl, then?" I breathed against her mouth.

A slow smile broke out over her face.

"Check and see," she invited.

I bent down until my mouth was only inches away from her pussy, and then gave one long, unhurried lick.

Her flavor burst on my taste buds, making my already hard cock practically strain the confines of my skin.

"Goddammit," I hissed. "You taste so good. I could get lost in everything that is you."

She shucked her shirt up and over her head, leaving her in nothing but a pair of rainbow ankle socks that looked absolutely adorable on her.

"Hurry or we'll be late," she insisted, holding her hands out to me.

I bent over her, putting all of my weight into my fisted hands on either side of her head.

"Guide me in," I told her.

She reached for my cock, and I had to close my eyes to keep from coming just at the feel of her hand around my straining erection.

"Don't," I said in a strangled groan when she pumped it twice.

She pumped one more time and my eyes nearly crossed at the pleasure that small hand could inflict on me.

Then she guided the ruddy head of my cock to her entrance, and I slowly pushed inside.

She gasped and arched, her belly meeting mine for a few long seconds as I sank deeply inside of her to the hilt.

"You feel so good," she breathed. "The first seconds after you enter me is like an electrocution to my nerve endings."

I couldn't agree more.

The way her tight heat practically clung to my invading cock was nothing short of life altering.

The alarm on my phone signaling it was time to leave sounded somewhere in the vicinity of the bathroom, and I caught Kitt's eyes.

"Hurry," she urged. "Give it to me fast!"

I wanted to laugh.

If I gave it to her how she wanted it, it'd literally be two point five seconds.

Which obviously she wanted when her heels started digging into my bare ass.

The waistband of my underwear dug into my ass as I started to hasten my thrusts.

One thrust. Two. Three.

She gasped and started to writhe underneath me.

"Oh God," she gasped.

Then I felt her pretty, wet pussy start to convulse, and I let go.

My release poured out of me, and I grunted with each spurt that burst from me.

"Jesus," she said, pushing at my chest. "You're heavy."

I went up to my knees and she gasped for breath.

Then started to laugh when she pointed to her stomach.

"Our daughter didn't like you taking any of her room," she pointed to her belly.

My cock instantly deflated as if it never was.

"Shit. Sorry," I said. "Gonna have to do that differently from now on."

She rolled her eyes and grabbed for her discarded t-shirt, placing it between her legs and waddling to the bathroom.

"You better hurry," she ordered, tossing me my phone that was still sounding its alarm.

I caught it and shut the alarm off.

Tossing it to the bed, I righted my underwear, smoothed out my shirt, yanked on my pants, and then shoved my feet into socks.

"Your boots are somewhere near the front door," she called when I started looking.

I smiled and ran to the bathroom, placing a soft kiss on her forehead where she stood brushing her teeth.

She leaned her head into me, and then said, "Go."

I did, stopping only long enough to grab my phone.

"Make sure you call me and let me know how the doctor's appointment went!" I called to her.

"Yes, sir!" She called. "Love you!"

I smiled and called, "Love you, too!"

Then I walked out the door, not knowing that later that day, I'd be receiving a call that would change my life.

***

Later that afternoon

"Licenses, please," I called to the two teenagers.

I eyed the empty beer cans in the bottom of the boat, then rolled my eyes when both boys looked at each other.

"We don't…have them with us right now," he lied.

I looked down at the thirty or so catfish on the stringer tied to the boat, and then back at the boys.

"Are y'all under sixteen?" I asked.

They both looked at each other again.

See, in the state of Texas, if you were under the age of sixteen, you didn't have to have a license to fish.

However, if you were sixteen, you definitely didn't want to be lying about not drinking all the beer that I could clearly tell they'd imbibed on.

"Listen," I said to the two boys that were obviously under the age of sixteen. In fact, if I had to guess, I'd say they were more along the age of fourteen or fifteen. "How about you call your parents. Have them come up here, and as long as all of those fish are legal, we'll not worry about it. Just make sure you ride home with them."

Both boys nodded their heads vigorously.

"Get them," I ordered.

Twenty minutes later, an obviously upset man and an equally upset mother hurried down the boat ramp to where the boys were still located.

Not even five seconds after seeing them, the woman started yelling.

The blonde kid winced and ducked his head, clearly not liking the fact that his mother was making such a big deal of it all. The father, though, was a different story.

He was watching the redheaded kid with an intensity so great that I almost felt sorry for the kid.

Almost.

"What has my son done?" He asked unhappily.

I relayed to him what I'd done and was just at the part where I was asking their ages when a familiar sounding motorcycle started to creep down the road.

I turned and nodded at Peek to let him know I saw him and turned back to my conversation.

"Your son and his friend decided to get drunk in a boat," I wanted to laugh as I explained this, but the moment I saw the father turn to the kid, his whole demeanor changed to one of extreme annoyance.

"Thank you. And what kind of…"

"*APPLE!*" Peek yelled.

My head whipped around and my stomach clenched at the emotion I saw etched into Peek's haggard face.

"Please make sure they don't drink and boat anymore, it could be just as detrimental as drinking and driving," I hurried, backing away and turning to run toward Peek.

My heart was beating fast in my chest as my face remained glued to Peek's expression.

"What?" I asked, my stomach now rolling.

He shook his head.

"Get in your truck. I'll drive."

I studied his face for a few long seconds then nodded, tossing him my keys.

If he didn't want me to drive, there was a reason.

And I had a feeling I knew exactly the reason for his abrupt arrival.

We were about two minutes into the drive when I finally got the nerve to ask.

"What happened to her?" I cleared my throat.

"Car wreck," he said. "The officer, Corey Capone, died at the scene. They rushed Kitt to the hospital with a severe head injury and some trauma to her lower body."

My eyes closed.

"And the baby?" I asked gruffly.

"I don't know."

The moment we arrived at the hospital my feet were moving me out of the truck and through the hospital doors that Peek parked about two feet away from.

"Apple!" Ridley caught me by the arm before I could barrel into the ER.

My head turned to study him.

His eyes were red from what looked like crying, and his hair was a fucking mess.

Which, for Ridley, was amazing in and of itself, seeing as he hated for his hair to be even a single strand out of place.

"Tell me," I demanded, grabbing a fistful of his shirt and pulling him to me.

He wrapped his arms around my larger frame and hugged me to him tightly.

"She's in surgery. Second floor. I'm just waiting on you. Let's go," he let me go.

We took the stairs up to the second floor.

I was so numb that I couldn't feel the way my heart pounded or the way my hands felt like ice.

Ridley walked up to the receptionist's desk and showed her his badge.

"Harrison County Sherriff. I'm here for Kitt Walker," he said.

The woman's eyes went from Ridley's face to her computer where her fingers quickly started to fly over the keyboard.

"She's still in surgery. If you would like to wait here I can go check with the nurse…"

"I'm her fiancé. She's having my baby. If you would do that, that would be good," I blurted, interrupting her explanation.

The woman smiled softly.

"I'll go check," she pushed back from her desk.

The woman went to stand, and I walked around the side of the desk to help her.

She had to be at least ninety, if not older.

But the old woman walked out the door and came back within five minutes.

"You have to stay here," she pointed at Ridley. "But you can come with me. She's been asking for you."

My eyes started to sting as I followed the old woman through the door behind her desk.

I looked back once at Ridley who looked torn.

I knew he wanted to come.

But he didn't want to make a big scene.

I gave him one grateful nod before the doors shut behind us.

"Which way?" I grated roughly.

She pointed.

"I'll take you, dear." She held my hand. "Don't want you getting lost."

I closed my eyes and tried not to scream at the old woman.

She was walking so goddamned slow that I was tempted to pick her the fuck up and ask her where to take her.

"She just got into surgery. She's been having seizure after seizure, and they've just now gotten those under control enough to sew her up, according to the doctor. The baby was delivered via C-section about five minutes ago," she recited.

I fought the urge to clench my hands, knowing in this state that I would likely break the old lady's bones.

"Apple Drew?" A woman asked, startling me.

I looked up and to the side to see a nurse in green scrubs outside a plain white door.

The old lady gave my hand one last squeeze before letting me go.

"Yes, ma'am," my voice cracked slightly.

She smiled at me.

"We were going to let you come in with her for a few moments, but she's completely under sedation now so she won't be able to speak to you," she said. "The baby, being seven and a half weeks early, will be taken to NICU. You may go with them, but you'll be asked to change into clean clothes and a gown."

She eyed the mud on my boots. "And I have some shoe covers we'd like you to put on."

I nodded my head.

"And Kitt? The baby? Are they okay?" I asked.

I must've sounded ravaged, because she gave me a soft smile.

"Both are okay," she promised. "The baby is healthy and had a forceful scream before I left her. She should be following me out…"

The door popped open behind her, and I heard the healthy set of lungs come out into the hallway.

My daughter, a red, screaming, covered in white goo, little bundle of pissed off came out of the door being pushed in a clear contraption by another nurse.

"Daddy?" The other nurse asked.

I nodded, my feet frozen to the floor.

"Mommy's doing okay," she grinned. "And this little one will likely be just fine, also. We're taking her to the NICU just in case, though."

I nodded mutely.

"Ready?" She asked, pushing my baby past the door in the direction of a bank of elevators.

I nodded, but still my feet wouldn't move.

"She's going to be just fine."

The nurse's words gave me the power to move, but only until my hand could touch the cool white door.

I closed my eyes and leaned my head against it, saying a prayer for the first time in over a year.

Don't leave me. Please fight.

My baby's whimper turned to a quiet hiccup, and I let my hand drop to my side.

"I'm ready."

CHAPTER 17

It's an 'I want to fake my death, move to Mexico and live on tequila and tacos' kind of day.
-Coffee Cup

Apple

"You're sure?" I asked the nurse.

She nodded.

"She needs the oxygen for now," she pointed to the mask that was over Emily's tiny nose. "You saw her chest?"

I nodded.

She'd been breathing fine at first, but over time, her breathing became labored. Her chest had started to cave inwards with the force of her breaths, and the NICU nurses and a doctor had immediately placed her on oxygen.

I studied her face, and her perfect little lips, so happy that all the malformations that the doctors said might be possible while Kitt was on her seizure meds didn't come to fruition.

She was a perfect little four-pound baby, and I wanted to hold her so badly I could scream.

"When will I get to hold her?" I asked, my finger running along

Emily's chest.

"Maybe tomorrow, once she's stable," the nurse answered. "We'll have to just wait and see. Babies, at this age, are so fragile, and we don't want to disturb her any more than we have to until we figure out just how healthy this baby is."

I nodded, understanding that it could be that way.

I'd done a lot of research on my phone and read about a hundred pamphlets while I'd been waiting on them to get her stabilized.

My phone buzzed, and I pulled it out of my pocket to see the text from Ridley.

Ridley (10:00 PM): No change. Still asleep.

My text was a picture of Emily with the oxygen nose shit taking up the entirety of her face.

Ridley's response made me snort.

Ridley (10:02): Looks like her mama. Same toes.

"All right, Mr. Apple," the nurse said sympathetically. "The NICU hours are from eight AM until eight PM. We're going to have to ask you to leave," she whispered apologetically.

I winced.

"Are you sure I have to leave?" My voice pleaded with her.

She nodded.

"I am. I'm sorry. But you can be here as soon as the clock strikes eight AM. I'll also be calling you if anything changes. You can also call me anytime you feel you need an update, okay?" She offered.

I nodded. "Yeah, okay."

With one last touch against Emily's cheek, I left the NICU feeling like I'd left my own beating heart behind.

I walked down one flight of stairs and turned left, following the directions I'd gotten from Ridley, arriving at Kitt's room and stopping in surprise when I saw not just Ridley inside, but Griffin and his wife, Mig and his wife, Casten and his wife, Peek and his wife, and Wolf.

They all stood the moment I came into the room.

"Pictures!" Lenore declared loudly.

I smiled and pulled out my phone, giving it to Lenore.

The other ladies quickly gathered around the phone and cooed over the pictures.

My eyes, however, were all for Kitt.

She looked swallowed in the big white hospital bed.

Her head had a huge laceration from the top of her hairline all the way down to her eyebrow.

Her leg was up in the air, wrapped from ankle to thigh.

The bedding was bunched up over her midsection, which looked weird not swollen with our child.

Her eyes were both black, and she had crusted, dried blood in her hair and around her ear.

I grabbed a washcloth from the sink, wet it and gently went to work on the blood.

I had to go rinse it at least three times before I was satisfied that it was all gone, and when I looked up next, the room was empty.

Taking a glance behind me to be sure, I closed my eyes.

Sighing in relief, I took a seat on the very edge of Kitt's bed, careful not to jostle her, and stared at her, willing her to wake.

"This wasn't how this was supposed to go," I told her, lifting my hand to brush a piece of her beautiful hair off her head. "You were supposed to have this kid naturally, and I was supposed to cut the umbilical cord. *What to Expect When You're Expecting* said so."

That beautiful laugh of hers didn't light up the air around me, and I closed my eyes as the tears that were clogging my throat threatened to spill over.

But then something she'd said a couple days back, the night I finally decided to pull my head out of my ass and tell her everything there was to know about me, good and bad, came back to me.

I love you. I love you when you're you. I love you when you're not you. I love you when you're sick. I love you when you're healthy. I'd take care of you even if you were a quadriplegic. You're it for me, and I'm it for you. Got it?

"I love you. I love you when you're you. I love you when you're not you. I love you when you're sick. I love you when you're healthy. I'd take care of you even if you were a quadriplegic. You're it for me, and I'm it for you. Got it?" I whispered.

She still didn't answer, but I wasn't worried. She'd come back to me. And when she did, she was mine.

Forever.

***

Day four after the accident Kitt woke with a vengeance.

"Get your hands off me, you stupid fool!" I heard yelled loudly. "Where's my baby!"

I rolled over from my back to my side and stared at the most beautiful vision I'd ever seen.

Kitt. Awake and pissed.

"Ma'am. Do you know where you are?" The nurse, the same one that'd been her nurse for the last two nights, asked her, ignoring her rude comments.

"I'm in the hospital, you twit," she said. "Even I can see that, and I don't know what day it is or how I got here. Now, take me to my baby!"

"Ma'am," the nurse tried to say. "I'll have to ask your doctor if it's okay for you to see the baby." She pointed to Kitt's leg that was still up in the contraption that kept it immobile. "He said we could take it down today, but I'll have to make sure before we do."

"You do that." Kitt snarled. "Now."

"I need to give you your medicines first," she informed her. "And we've been pumping your breast milk for your baby every two hours. Which is another thing I was in here to do."

"Who would give you permission to do something like that?" Kitt hissed. "Isn't that a sexual violation?"

"Kitt," my deep, resonate voice said softly. "Don't."

Kitt's head snapped sideways, and her eyes widened.

"You," she hissed. "What did you do to me?"

I wanted to laugh.

I didn't dare.

"I gave her permission to do that, otherwise we would've had to see if we could find a milk bank that would supply Emily's meals for her," I sat up and placed my feet flat on the floor.

Kitt's eyes narrowed.

"You named our child Emily?" She screeched, eyes narrowing. "Who gave you permission to do that?"

I stood, keeping my eyes on her.

"Can you come back in thirty minutes?" I asked the nurse. "I'll do the milking."

Kitt's gasp of outrage followed the nurse out, and she glared at me with venom in her eyes.

"Did you just say you were going to milk me?" She asked with a snarl. "Like a fucking cow?"

I bent over so my arms were on either side of her hips and turned my head so I could see her face straight on.

"I did. What are you going to do about it?" I asked, moving so close to her that all I could see were her eyes.

"I'm going to let you," she whispered. "But I'm not going to be happy about it."

I wanted to laugh.

"I will," I suppressed my grin. "Because I like touching your boobs."

She gave up the ghost and threw her head back and laughed.

"You remembered that I wanted to call her Emily?" She asked once she composed herself.

I nodded.

"What'd you use as her middle name?" She wondered.

I grinned. "Ryan."

"Emily Ryan Drew?" Her eyes went dreamy.

"Yeah," I said. "I liked it."

"That sounds good. But my brother's going to get a big head," she pursed her lips.

"Ridley Ryan Walker was already taken," my brother said from the door. "So we had to settle for Emily. Why you'd want to name our baby after our mother is beyond me."

I snorted.

Ridley and Kitt's mother wasn't the nicest of people, from what I'd heard. She'd been strict and overbearing, and had died with their father when they were teenagers during a traffic accident.

They'd lived with their grandfather until the age of eighteen when he decided they were old enough to live on their own. The next day he moved into a nursing home two states up from them and refused to come home anymore because he liked the fishing in Tennessee too much.

If they were going to name the baby after anyone, it should have been their grandfather.

Not the mother.

But who knew the mind of a woman, anyway?

CHAPTER 18

Porn is bullshit. How the hell do they have sex without the fitted sheet popping off?
-Text from Ridley to Apple

Kitt

I stared at Apple as he broke through yet another large log with his massive axe, and my loins clenched with need.

I looked over at Perry, Apple's father.

"Do you think you could watch her for a couple of minutes," I pleaded.

Perry looked over from his position, glancing at Emily where she was swinging in her new, state of the art swing, and nodded.

"I can," he agreed, his voice slurred slightly.

I smiled and stood, taking a hesitant step on my now cast-free foot.

"Thank you," I murmured before heading in Apple's direction.

Today, I'd had three appointments.

One for my OB checkup, stating I was now cleared to have all the sex I wanted. The second to have my cast removed from my leg. And the third was an appointment with my seizure doc who put me on a different regimen of meds.

My phone rang when I was just about to go down the steps, and I glared at it once I read the readout.

"Hello?" I asked shortly.

"Hi, Kitt!" Jake sang. "I noticed you weren't home, and I was just calling to check on you!"

I gritted my teeth, so close to telling the guy to go fuck himself that it wasn't even funny.

"I'm fine, Jake," I growled through clenched teeth. "Bye."

I hung up and glared at my phone, shoving it back into my pocket in favor of throwing it.

"Who was that?" Apple asked, taking another swing of the axe.

I watched as his body rippled and bunched. Then I watched as he bent over, grabbed the wood that was piled up on either side of his chopping block and tossed it aside to the huge pile that was even further away.

I lost count of how many logs he'd split today.

This morning, I'd looked out the window and had seen what looked like a whole freakin' tree ready to be cut up.

And I'd arrived to it all in sections, and the majority of it cut up into firewood.

"How long have you been going?" I asked him. "Have you taken a break at all?"

He looked at me over his shoulder, his face dripping with sweat.

His beard was curlier than usual due to the moisture on his face, and it made him look even more rugged than I was used to from him.

His gray t-shirt was clinging to the planes of his chest and back, and his jeans had a ring of sweat right around the waist that went down past his ass.

His arms were covered in small pieces of wood chips, and his glasses had small particles clinging to them, too.

"Since you left," he panted. "I have two pieces left, and I'm done."

He indicated the two larger logs that he had left to be split, and I sighed.

Taking one long glance behind me at Perry, I slipped past the house so he couldn't see anymore but Apple could, and stared at Apple until he turned to me.

Once I had his eyes, I hooked my fingers in the hem of my shirt, and then ripped it up and off my head.

His eyes bugged as he took a quick glance behind him, and then back to me.

"Put it back on," he ordered gruffly.

I shook my head.

"Can't," I disagreed. "The doctor cleared me for sex. Either you give it to me, or I go take care of it myself like old times."

His eyes narrowed. "I'm almost done. I'll come up there when I'm finished."

He was trying hard, I'd give him that.

In fact, he'd been a good boy for going on two months now.

He'd been kicking his ass as he tried to make everyone happy.

He helped me with Emily. He helped me out even more when a seizure would knock me down on my ass. He helped Ridley. He helped his father. He helped other game wardens who were sick, picking up the odd shift for other areas here and there.

And then there was the wood splitting when he was home and he wasn't needed elsewhere.

Needless to say, I was getting sick and tired of him taking care of everyone but himself.

"Apple," I said, my tone biting.

Apple's eyes, already focused on me but not my face, snapped up to mine.

"Yeah?" He gasped, chest still heaving.

"You either come up here now, or I'll go home with Emily and not come back for the night."

His eyes narrowed.

"Are you giving me an ultimatum here?" He warned.

I nodded.

"Yes," I nodded sharply. "Either you give me what I want, or I leave."

"You won't leave me," he ordered.

I wanted to laugh.

I wouldn't leave him. But I'd go home and stop watching his sexy body as he worked his ass off.

Then he'd follow me home later, and I'd already be in bed.

Which he wouldn't wake me from.

Not if he could help it.

The only way he'd actually wake me was if Emily needed to be fed and I didn't hear her crying, but I always heard her.

So he wouldn't have that excuse, and he'd have to leave me alone because he was too scared of being the cause of one of my seizures.

I lifted my finger and watched him watch me.

His eyes staying glued to mine.

I could tell he wanted to drop those eyes and watch my fingers circle my pebbled nipples, but he didn't.

He kept watching my eyes, *intently*.

Knowing he'd follow if I left, I turned my back on him and walked to the barn where he no longer lived.

He'd moved in with us mostly. His stuff was still in the barn, but most of his clothes were now housed in my closet.

His shoes took up the underside of my bed.

His guns took up a shelf in my bathroom closet.

I stocked his favorite cookies, Oreos, in my pantry.

For all intents and purposes, he was now moved into the house with me, Emily and Ridley.

Although Ridley rarely saw him.

When Ridley was there, Apple was at work. When Apple was there, Ridley was at work.

I wasn't even sure if Ridley knew exactly what was going on with Apple and me.

It looked poorly that every time Ridley walked in the door, Apple was walking out of it.

And not all of those times was Apple working.

Sometimes he was chopping wood like he was doing now. Others he was just walking out the door to walk out the door, and I wanted to know why.

Emily had been home with us for a little over four weeks now, and of those four weeks, I might have seen Apple for a whole four hours of it.

He was there, but he wasn't *there*.

And I wanted to know why.

Which was why I was ambushing him today.

He either gave me what I wanted, or I went all crazy on him and started making a big deal of it when I really didn't want to.

I made it to the top of the steps before I heard the barn door creak open below.

I was bending over the bed, my hands on the checkered cotton sheets, when I felt Apple's hands on my hips, pulling me against his hard erection that was tenting the front of his jeans.

I didn't even care that those jeans were covered in sweat and wood chips.

I was ecstatic that he was even acknowledging that I was there.

"I'm tired," he grunted softly.

I looked at him over my shoulder, my brows furrowed.

"You don't want to do this?" I asked carefully.

His eyes went up my naked body, starting at my bare ass and ending at the top of my shoulder blades.

"Oh, I want this," he said. "But I want to do this at home, later tonight, in our own bed."

I was shaking my head before he even finished.

"Absolutely not," I denied, breaking away from his hold and turning around on the bed. "You're going to lay there and let me love you."

His eyes flared.

"I am not," he contradicted. "We can't leave Emily with my dad. He can't take care of her."

I narrowed my eyes.

"I left my cell phone on the table with him, and a bottle ready to feed her the moment—*and that's a big if since I just fed her not even an hour ago*—she wakes up," I said. "And you need to stop coddling us and let us breathe."

"I'm not coddling you!" He replied, angry now. "I'm *protecting* you!"

"Protecting us from what?" I asked, throwing my arms out wide. "Ourselves?"

His eyes narrowed.

"Every time you get excited you have a fucking seizure that knocks you out for half a day. Excuse fucking me if I'm trying to prevent that," he hissed, backing away from the bed.

I followed him, being careful of my still weak leg when I stepped.

"That sounds like a bitch excuse to me," I goaded him. "It sounds like you're keeping me in a goddamned bubble that I can't fucking breathe inside. Do you know what it's like to be told to do *nothing*?"

"Most girls would like that their man takes care of them," he muttered darkly.

My brows rose again.

"Most girls aren't me. I'm independent. I like being able to go to places I want to go. Such as the grocery store or Wal-Mart to buy my own goddamned Kotex."

He crossed his arms.

"I did that for you!" He snapped, instantly upset that I would say he didn't provide for me.

"I know you did. That's the problem," I muttered. "I want to do stuff. Take Emily to a mommy and me class."

"She's still too young," he said instantly.

I sighed, pinching the bridge of my nose.

"I know that," I groaned.

"Then why would you just say you wanted to take her to a mommy and me class when you know she's too young for that?" He questioned.

"It was an example!" I fumed. "I want to go places. On a date. With you! I've never even been on a date with you that my brother didn't orchestrate."

His eyes went intense.

"What are you talking about?" He hesitated.

I smiled at him and not in a nice way.

"You didn't think I'd find out that my brother asked you to take me on a date?" I smiled, and not in a good way. "Well, you'd be mistaken."

I prowled forward, letting him see the hurt in my eyes.

The same hurt that was in my eyes this morning when I heard my brother joking around with Wolf, saying he was the reason Emily was even alive. That if it hadn't been for him, the most beautiful girl in the world wouldn't have even been conceived.

"I took you out because I wanted to take you out," he said stiffly. "Had I not already been planning that event, I wouldn't have said yes to your brother."

I glared at him.

"How am I ever supposed to trust that?" I cracked, throwing my hands up in despair. "I was a pity date!"

He was on me before I even finished bringing my hands back down to my sides.

"Pity?" He shook his head, grabbing a hold of my chin with one large hand. "I don't fucking pity you for what you think I pity you for."

"What?" I asked in confusion.

The 'what' came out sounding more like 'waft' since his hand was impeding my ability to speak clearly.

But it got the point across.

"I pity you because you have to deal with me for the rest of your life," he leveled with me.

I blinked.

"Why would you pity me for that for?" I wondered. "That actually sounds like heaven to me."

He backed away with disgust.

"How can you say that?" He ran his hands through his sweat slickened hair. "I've ruined your fucking life."

I looked at him with incredulity.

"Ummm. How?" I was lost.

He looked at me like I'd grown a second head and then started pacing.

"Emily is mine and yours. You'll forever have to deal with me, even when you wise up and decide I'm not worth the trouble," he muttered, his hands going up to cup the back of his neck.

"I don't see that happening any time soon. Plus, I thought we discussed this. That you were it for me," I told him gently, taking a seat on the bed when my noodle leg started to shake from the exertion of standing up for so long.

He turned his head to look at me, then turned back to the wall where he was staring as he paced.

"Why do you think I'm still here?" He questioned. "I made you a promise, and even though I think that promise was stupid on your part, I'll stay. Because you asked me to. And because I'm too selfish to go."

I pinched the bridge of my nose again.

"Have you been taking your meds?" I tilted my head slightly, seeing where this was going.

He looked over at me sharply.

"I…ran out." he confessed. "I have to go get them refilled."

I sighed in exasperation.

"You're stupid," I grunted. "Jesus Christ, you can't just stop taking those. They're making you better."

He shrugged.

"I've been too busy."

Because of me. And Emily.

"I gotta go," I picked up my clothes from the floor and dropped them on the bed.

Before I could tell him that he was leaving with me, though, Apple was on me, turning me over onto my back and following me down.

"You're not leaving me," he declared. "You're mine. And I never let go of what's mine."

I blinked.

"I wasn't letting you go," I cupped his face. "You were coming with me."

He blinked, his beautiful eyes staring deeply into mine.

"I'm not ready to leave just yet." His voice dropped.

"Then what are you ready to do?" I asked breathlessly.

He ground his erection between my legs, and I blinked at him, then asked cheekily. "You want to dance?"

He growled and reached a hand between us to unbutton and unzip his pants.

Shoving them down, and then kicking them off completely, he came up to his haunches between my legs, and then pushed his erection down on top of my slit.

I arched when his length touched my clit, and then started to moan when he thrust his hips, letting the length rub against me. Coating himself in my juices that'd accumulated while I'd been watching his beautiful body chop wood.

"You're ready for me," he observed, bringing his hand that was now covered in the essence of me up to his lips.

Then his tongue slipped out between those perfectly white teeth and he licked his hand clean.

"Jesus Christ," he groaned. "You taste so good."

My eyes went molten as I spread my legs wider.

"Fuck me," I ordered him.

He leaned down and positioned his erection at my entrance, then slowly slid inside.

"Oh, God," I whispered, my eyes closing as he filled me. "You feel bigger."

He chuckled darkly as he bent forward and captured my lips with his.

"Not bigger," he promised. "You're just tighter."

"I don't know why…or how," I admitted, eyes closing as his strokes started to pick up in speed.

His hands moved to capture my thighs, hooking the backs of my knees over his forearms, as he pulled out and then slammed inside.

I squeaked in surprise as he hit bottom, inside of me.

"Good or bad?" He slowed.

"Good," I panted. "Hurry. Faster. Now."

He growled in approval and started the same rhythm back up. All the way out until his cock rested at my entrance, then he thrust inside so fast and hard that I could barely breathe.

The oxygen deprivation was perfectly fucking acceptable, though. At that moment in time, I wouldn't have noticed a damn thing was happening to me because my body was too focused on what he was doing between my legs.

Between one thrust and the next I was coming, bursting apart into a million tiny pieces of Kitt, as my orgasm took hold.

My eyes closed, as well as crossed, as I felt him stiffen inside of me.

His cock twitched, and I was only aware just enough to hear him curse as his warmth bathed my insides.

My pussy clenched as I came with him, my breath coming in short pants.

Needless to say, the previous couple of minutes went about as I'd intended them to—only earlier. I now had him exactly where I wanted him.

Forever.

Sadly, life had a way of intervening into our perfect world as reality came back.

We were lying in the bed, panting and about ready to pass out from the exertion, when I said the words that I didn't know Apple needed to hear.

"I want to get married."

"Just say when, and I'll be there," he declared. "Do you want your ring now or after we go to the store to refill my prescription."

I laughed at him.

"Now. Then we need to go do that. And you need to not run out again," I said. "What would you say if I did the same thing?"

He growled at me.

"Point taken."

I smiled.

Then we went to the store, where we *both* refilled our prescriptions.

Yep, perfectly fucked up together.

That night I had another seizure.

And the night after that.

And the night after that.

And the day after that.

Which caused my brother to wreck his new truck, and everyone to begin questioning what exactly *was* wrong with me, and if I'd ever have a normal life again.

CHAPTER 19

A king only bows down to his queen.
-Apple to Ridley

Apple

I ran through the hospital doors, Emily in my arms, praying that Kitt would be all right.

Again.

This was beginning to be a habit that I seriously didn't enjoy.

At least this time I had one less person to worry about seeing as Emily was currently in my arms.

I wasn't worried about Ridley at all.

He'd been the one to call me to tell me that they'd been in the accident in the first place, so it was natural not to be as worried when he sounded perfectly fine.

The second I passed through the ER doors, I walked immediately to where Kitt and Ridley were in beds next to each other, hurrying to them.

"Here," I gave Emily to Ridley, not caring that one of his arms was hurt.

I also didn't care that the movement would likely cause my kid to puke. Something she'd already done in the truck on the way.

Over the last two months we'd been very careful when it came to moving Emily around after she'd been fed. If we weren't careful, then the movement made Emily puke, and we'd have to feed her all over again.

My body turned, allowing me to survey Kitt's injuries.

She was awake and conscious, and I knew that she wasn't in a good place.

"You scared the shit out of me," I blurted. "And Emily puked all over the back of the truck."

Her mouth curved up at the edges, and a smile broke out over her face.

It was the most beautiful sight in the world.

Walking carefully toward her, I sat down on the edge of her hospital bed and stared deeply into her eyes.

"I don't like what your eyes are telling me," I told her softly.

She looked haunted, and I didn't like that. Not even a little bit.

Not when that haunted look would normally mean very bad things if it'd been reversed and on my face.

"Talk to me, momma," I said softly.

Her eyes closed, and then reopened.

"I'm a menace to society," she whispered brokenly.

"How do you figure?" I asked.

She swallowed hard.

"I killed Corey," she whispered. "I almost killed my baby." She scrubbed her hands over her face. "And I almost killed my brother today. And I'm only getting worse!"

I caught her hand that had flailed out to the side and brought it up to my lips.

"You're not a menace to society," I said. "And I think it's time for a second opinion. You've been with this doctor in Dallas for a while now, and I think it's time to use someone else's knowledge and hope that maybe they can find the answers that your other doctor can't."

She closed her eyes.

"And what if they don't have any idea, either?" She whispered brokenly.

I was about to reply when Kitt's face turned to her brother and she snapped, "Language!"

I turned too, noticing that the floor was covered in spit up and that a nurse had quite a bit of it dripping down her pant leg into her shoe.

Ridley's eyes were focused on the nurse like a predator, and I sat there, stunned, to see anything other than indifference on his face when it came to a woman.

"Apple."

I turned back to Kitt, raising my brow at her.

"What?" I asked.

"You didn't answer. What if the other doctor doesn't have any idea, either?" She pushed.

"Then we worry about that when it happens. Don't borrow trouble."

***

Kitt

Two days later, I found myself at my new doctor's office.

"Hello, dear. It's nice to meet you. Would you come in?" My new doctor, Dr. Pierce, smiled and waved his hand for me to enter.

We both followed him in and took seats directly across the desk from him.

My belly was turning as I stared at him.

The nurse that my daughter had puked on last night had recommended Dr. Pierce, and he'd worked me in the very next morning.

After reviewing my chart, he'd called and asked me to meet him at his office at eight this morning. I was also instructed not to take any of my medications and to eat normally with no caffeine intake.

So I'd done as instructed, and now here I sat, tired and nervous as hell, Apple at my side.

Then again, that's where he'd been since my accident yesterday morning.

Apple, somehow sensing my thoughts were on him, grabbed my hand and squeezed it lightly, giving me strength that I didn't know I needed.

I gave him a quick smile, letting him know that I was alright and turned back to the doctor who was shuffling papers around on his desk.

"I had the nurse pull your blood work from the accident two months ago, and the blood work from yesterday, as well as the last set of blood work we ran on you about a month prior to finding out that you were pregnant," he started.

I nodded.

He continued after making sure I comprehended where he was.

"Your hormone levels are back to normal," he said.

"If that's the case, why in the hell is she still having seizures since that was the previous doctor's only guess as to why she was having the seizures during her pregnancy?" Apple asked.

There was no beating around the bush for Apple. The man was like a bull in a china shop when it came to getting information that he wanted or needed.

"I'm getting there," he said, holding up a finger. "I've got some good news and some not so good news," he proceeded.

"Okay," I cleared my throat. "What's the bad news?"

He smiled.

"The medication you've been taking since you had your daughter hasn't been correct. In fact, it's not even a little bit correct. The pharmacy misread the doctor's handwriting and has been giving you something that's supposed to control anxiety, not your seizures, which is why you've had poor success with this medication regimen."

My mouth dropped open.

Surely I hadn't heard him correctly, right?

But he wasn't laughing.

Not even a little bit.

And the man at my side sure wasn't laughing.

"You're telling me she hasn't been getting the correct medications all this time?" Apple asked in outrage.

The doctor held his hand up.

"Yes and no," he said.

Apple narrowed his eyes. "Explain."

Dr. Pierce held up his hand. "First, I want to know what your diet was like when you were pregnant."

I blinked, turning to survey him more completely.

"Normal, I guess. I ate fruit and or oatmeal in the morning. Normally, a sandwich and chips for lunch, and whatever we had for dinner. Pizza. Meat loaf. I didn't cut out any foods or anything. Why?" I asked.

"What kind of fruit?" Dr. Pierce asked.

I shrugged.

"Sometimes oranges. Grapefruit mostly. That seemed to be the one thing I craved throughout the pregnancy," I murmured. "Grapes were a third favorite."

Something in his body changed, and I knew something in the explanation I'd just given him had been the cause of that change.

"Grapefruit is contraindicated to take with your seizure meds you were on," he explained. "Didn't your previous doctor explain that?"

"I know," I nodded. "That's what the nurse kept telling me every time she gave me some pamphlets and sample drugs when I visited their office."

He winced.

"Contraindicated is not a good thing. Contraindicated means you should not be taking, using or eating them with the meds that you were on," he explained gently.

My belly dropped out from under me as I stared at him in shock.

"So you're telling me I did this all to myself?" I gasped in shock.

He shook his head.

"No," he held up his hand. "That's not what I said. What I'm trying to explain is that the grapefruit juice interacts with the medication impairing the way they respond in your body. They don't necessarily render them completely ineffective, though. Pairing the ineffectiveness of the meds with the hormone levels and adding in the changes in you during your pregnancy, it only exacerbated the issues you already had."

I shook my head.

"What about the meds after she had the baby?" Apple broke in. "You said she was getting the wrong meds. And I know for a fact that she stopped eating grapefruit nearly the instant she had Emily."

"Her system showed a high dose of an anti-anxiety medication. Normally, the two alone would both treat the disorder, but when combined they counteracted each other, changing the levels of the medicine her body would need to treat the seizures in the first place," he said. "Essentially, she wasn't getting enough medication, and the more seizures she had, the more she exacerbated the problem, causing even more seizures to happen."

We sat there, silent, as we processed that information.

"So what now?" I finally asked when I couldn't come up with anything else to say.

"Now, we wean you off the medicines completely. I want to see how you do without any medicine at all," he answered.

I nodded.

"Then what?" I asked.

"Then we'll see."

CHAPTER 20

And I was like 'whatever bitches' and the bitches whatevered.
-E-card

Kitt

"Do you mind packing me a lunch?" Apple asked me. "I'm running late as fuck this morning."

He ripped off the shirt that Emily had just projectile vomited on and started hurrying for the bedroom all the while Ridley looked on with laughing eyes.

"You're such a shithead," I told my brother.

My brother shrugged unrepentantly. "I'm just glad it wasn't me."

I grunted and walked to the counter, easily making him two peanut butter and jelly sandwiches.

The next thing to go onto the counter was a large thermos of milk. I wasn't sure if he packed that or not, but I knew when he was at home, he had milk with his sandwiches.

I followed the two sandwiches up with a Ziploc bag of barbeque chips and a banana.

"Will you grab me a bag out of there?" I asked Ridley.

Ridley grabbed a Wal-Mart sack out of the cabinet where we kept them and tossed it at me.

It went about half the distance it should've gone, meaning it fell to my feet.

I sighed and picked it up off the floor and stood up to find Ridley holding the banana in one hand with a Sharpie in the other.

"What are you writing on that?" I asked warningly.

Ridley grinned and tossed the banana into the bag, which I immediately took out and read.

"Seriously?" I asked him.

He shrugged.

"I don't see the big deal," he said.

"*You put this banana to shame*," I read the banana. "You think that's acceptable to put on a man's banana?"

We both paused for long seconds before we both burst out laughing.

Shoving the banana in the bag with the chips, sandwiches, and thermos of milk, I tied it shut and held it out just as Apple came rushing in.

"It's time," Apple agreed shrugging on a fresh shirt. "And you need to tell that jackwad Jake not to call anymore or I'll kick his fucking ass."

I snorted.

Calling Jake a 'jackwad' was an understatement. I would classify him more as a rodent. Or a roach.

I was seriously tired of answering the man's phone calls. The more he called, the less polite I was.

If he called me today, let's just say that I wouldn't be responsible for what I did.

"I'll handle it," Ridley promised.

"Thanks, baby," Apple said as he took the sack from my hand.

With a quick peck on my lips he exited the kitchen through the garage.

Short seconds later I heard the roar of his engine rumble to life, and then he was gone.

"What's he got going today?" Ridley questioned as he started to make his own lunch.

He grabbed the leftover steak and potatoes from yesterday's dinner and tucked it under his arm.

"Something about a presentation at the wildlife refuge," I told him. "And he has to meet his superior in Longview for lunch."

He stopped, eyebrows rising.

"And who's staying with you?" He demanded.

I grinned.

"I'm staying by myself!" I grinned excitedly.

His eyes went wary, and then he looked to the video monitors we'd just canceled the service for yesterday, and then back to me.

"Are you sure that's wise?" He asked warily.

I nodded.

"It is," I agreed. "It's time."

It'd been three months and some change since I'd stopped my medication completely and not one single time had I had a seizure.

Not. Freaking. Once.

And I'd never in my life been more ecstatic.

Well, kind of.

Last week, Emily had mastered the art of sitting up all by herself, and I had to say, that was a pretty exciting day in the Drew/Walker household.

"I won't be able to come check on you today. I will be busy all day," Ridley glared.

My brows rose.

"Hot date?" I asked him teasingly.

I knew he had a crush on the cute little nurse that we'd met at the hospital those few short months ago, but he'd been really secretive about it.

"Not exactly," he hedged. "I'll discuss it with you and Apple when I get home," his lips thinned. "Give that kid to me so I can give her a kiss."

I handed her over, watching with happiness in my eyes as he gave her a sloppy wet kiss that she thought was the best thing in the entire world.

She giggled a deep belly laugh that was like tinkling bells to my ears, and then passed her back to me.

"Be good," he narrowed his eyes. "And, swear to God, you get into trouble today, I'm never forgiving you."

I snorted.

"Yes, dad."

He pointed at me with a stiffened finger.

"Careful, kid."

I raised my hands in a haunted fashion.

"I'm shaking in my boots."

***

I sat on the couch, stunned.

"You're…joking, right?" I asked my brother who'd just dropped a fucking bombshell on us.

He blinked, and then shook his head.

"No. Not kidding," he said. "Our brother's a fucking dumbass, and I have to fix this."

I was shaking my head before he'd even finished.

"You don't have to fix a goddamned thing that that stupid man has done," I hissed. "He's no one to us. No one."

Ridley's lips tightened.

"It's not just about Connor," he murmured softly. Taking a deep breath, he released it and then glanced at Apple before turning back to me. "This has everything to do with the stupid mother fucker, Hanson Coller."

The name Hanson Coller sent ice through my veins.

"Apple," I interrupted. "Can you give me a few minutes with

Ridley alone?"

Apple glanced at me, then to Ridley, before nodding.

"Yeah," he agreed. "I'll give you a few. I'll get Emily ready for bed."

With that he was gone, and I was left staring at my brother.

"You're going to put your foot into it, and it's going to backfire on not just you, but that nurse you're trying to hide that you're seeing," I said softly.

His eyes, already haunted with demons from his past, clouded over more.

"Don't worry about her."

I rolled my eyes.

"I hope you know what you're doing," my breath hitched.

He looked over at me, and his eyes trailed over my face, down to my hands that were wringing together in my lap, then back up to my eyes.

"I do," he promised.

I got up, and he followed suit.

He opened his arms, and I walked straight into them.

He hugged me tight, gave me one last kiss on the forehead and then let me go before saying, "Now go to Apple and fill him in on my life story so I don't have to."

I snorted and punched him lightly in the gut.

"Yes, dad."

He smacked me upside the head.

Softly, but still.

"Watch it," I warned him with a pointed finger.

He winked and I grinned, going upstairs with my belly rolling at knowing what my brother was about to do.

"Shit."

"What?" Apple asked, startling me.

I gasped and turned just in time to be gathered into Apple's arms.

"Emily's down for the night. You okay?"

I shook my head.

"My brother's doing something stupid," I whispered back to him.

"Ridley's not Connor," he said.

I nodded.

And I knew that.

Connor was Ridley's twin, and my older brother. A brother that I didn't know well, because Ridley protected me from him.

A brother that I only had bad memories of, and I never thought about because he wasn't much of a brother to me at all and had been even less of a brother to Ridley.

Meaning, I barely, if ever, thought about him.

And, if I was being honest, didn't want to talk about him, either.

I'd given Apple the details of my brother months ago during a conversation that came up about Emily's living family members.

So Apple knew that Connor wasn't a beloved member of our family. That Connor had terrorized Ridley all because he could and there was no love lost between us.

"I know," I said to Apple. "Let's go to bed."

Apple picked me up around the waist and took me into our room, laying me gently down onto the bed before following me down.

"You happy, pretty girl?" He looked into my eyes.

"I was until my brother told me he was going to go undercover in a prison to try to get back at the man that was responsible for killing his wife," I conceded.

Apple kissed me full on my lips, and then leaned back far enough to look into my eyes.

My breathing was faster, and my heart was definitely pounding, just from one tiny little kiss.

Apple had the power to undo me, though, and I found that I quite liked that.

"Let's go to bed," he ordered roughly, pulling me to my feet so we could both strip out of our clothes.

I followed him to the bathroom, tossing my puke stained shirt into the hamper.

He waited until I was inside before pushing the door closed.

The moment the door latched behind me I found myself with my back pressed up against the wall, my legs wrapped around Apple's hips.

"Condoms," I breathed. "We need condoms."

"Got it," he growled against my lips, licking along the seam.

My eyes closed and my mouth dropped open, surrendering to his advances.

"You're sure about this?" I asked him. "I…"

"I'm sure," he shut me up with a kiss. "Tomorrow, I go in to get it done. And then we'll start planning."

"Planning for what?" I tilted my head back to give him full access to the length of my exposed neck.

"Then you and me plan the rest of our lives together," he said, unzipping his jeans and shoving his pants down his legs.

His underwear soon followed, and the crinkle of foil sounded amongst our deep breathing.

Giggling when he was about to kneel between my legs, I rolled and sat up, pointing to the bed as I did.

"I'm on top," I said, shucking my nightgown up and pushing my panties off, going on one knee at a time to untangle them from around my feet.

He snorted and hooked me around the waist, falling down to the bed with me, his front to my back.

"Lift your leg up," he ordered.

I did as instructed, bending my leg up and lifting it to my chest as he grabbed hold of his cock and placed it at my entrance.

I was moaning the moment he worked the head of his cock inside.

By the time he was about half way in, my eyes were squeezing shut.

The angle of his cock entering me meant the tip was rubbing against that certain spot inside of me that was sure to make me wild, and he knew it.

Which was why he was taking short strokes, running the head along my g-spot before pulling back out again.

"Jesus," he whispered, dropping his head to my shoulder. "You better find it quick."

I didn't need to find it. It was already there.

I was just on the brink of it when I heard Emily's cry from the other room.

"Dammit," I gasped, my orgasm waning.

Apple felt it and rolled us, yanking my hips up so I was on my hands and knees, my shoulders still flat against the bed.

And he started fucking me.

Not short strokes, either. Long. Hard. Rough.

My eyes squeezed shut as that waning orgasm was brought back to life with a vengeance.

"Don't know why I would think long and slow would work with us," Apple grumbled, his hands convulsing on my hips when my pussy started to ripple.

My orgasm shattered through me, my breath bursting out of my lungs like a punch to the stomach.

Emily's cry sounded again, more pissed off this time, and Apple stiffened behind me.

He grunted as his release rushed through him, causing his breath to leave his lungs.

“Fuck me,” I whispered, coming down moments later.

“Already did, darlin’,” Apple teased, pulling out of me quickly.

I giggled and rolled, scooting off the bed and grabbing my panties from the floor.

I bent over to slip my feet into the holes, and Apple took advantage of the position and slapped my ass on the way to the bathroom to dispose of the condom.

“She’s yours,” I yelled at him.

“No she’s not,” he disagreed. “I don’t have the tits. You do.”

I snorted and walked out of the room, rolling my eyes as I got to Emily’s door and saw her staring at me like I’d betrayed her.

“Don’t look at me like that!” I ordered her, reaching down into her crib for her. “Your daddy’s the one who put you in here!”

She latched onto my hair as Apple spoke from the doorway.

“Had we not put her in here, she would’ve woken up, and you would’ve demanded I stop fucking you,” he drawled.

I tossed him a venomous look over my shoulder and got that heart-stopping grin of his in return.

“Sit down and feed her again so we can go to bed,” he ordered, pointing to the chair.

I sighed, then took a seat and started feeding Emily.

Emily, my sweet baby girl who liked to vomit just for the hell of it, was a grazer.

She suckled on and off for a bit, like the true snacker that she was. Which meant what it always did, I'd be feeding her again. Often.

Another reason why she had yet to sleep through the night.

And was also why Apple had demanded we put her into her own room just a few short days ago.

She needs to learn that you're not going to come at the drop of a hat, he'd instructed.

So that's what we did. And now I had to wake the hell up completely instead of pulling her from her bed into ours and then putting her back in hers once I was done.

Granted, it was a little worrisome trying to make love to Apple when she was there, but we'd made it work.

We'd gotten hella creative, that was for sure.

"She's asleep," Apple mumbled. "Put her up and let's go to bed."

My eyes went from Emily's cheek to Apple, who'd watched me feed her for the short time that she actually ate before she fell asleep like usual.

This was a nightly ritual. We'd put her down for the night, and she'd wake up within the hour, demand a fill up and then go right back to sleep for another four hours.

Hopefully longer tonight, I thought morosely as I laid her down into the crib, then fixed my shirt to cover my breast once again.

"Hate that part," Apple came up behind me and caged me in with his arms along the top rail of Emily's crib.

I turned to look up at him, placing my hands on top of his.

"When you cover that pretty titty up," he teased, rubbing his beard along the side of my face.

I cupped his chin, letting my fingers trail along the beard that was trimmed down once again.

I loved his beard. I loved it short. I loved it long. I loved it trimmed. I just loved it, period.

The way he was wearing it now, a bit on the shorter side, though, was my ultimate favorite. It let me see his face while still enjoying all the benefits of having a beard.

Like the way he trailed his beard along the inside of my thigh just before he put his mouth on me.

Or the way he'd rub it against my neck in the morning to wake me up.

Or the way Emily pulled on it when she was in his arms and wanted his attention.

Now, with his beard pressed against my neck, our eyes on Emily, I couldn't think of a better feeling I'd ever experienced.

This was what I'd been searching for my entire life.

Something I'd always wanted but had never had, not even with my parents.

No, this was something not everyone got. Something so special that you remembered it, thought back on it, for years to come. This one special moment in time would be forever ingrained in my memory.

"You ready for bed, baby?" He asked when he sensed I wasn't going to reply to his earlier comment.

I nodded.

"I am."

And as I laid in Apple's arms that night, thinking about how much my life had changed for the better, I sent a silent prayer up to the sky.

Thank you for giving me everything I've ever wanted in life. Watch over them, please.

And three hours and fifty-seven minutes later, after feeding Emily, I came back to bed and curled back into Apple's arms.

Everything was right in my world.

***

Jake

I narrowed my eyes as my woman curled into another man's arms.

Crying and moaning sounded from beside me, and I turned to glare at the bitch that most certainly was not Kitt but would do for now.

"Shut it, bitch," I hissed, liking the way her mascara smeared when she cried.

She swallowed convulsively, but the tears still fell, and I smiled.

"You want me?" I stood up and stalked in her direction.

She started to shake her head, but I grabbed her hair before she could say no.

As long as they didn't say the word 'no', it wasn't wrong. That's what the law said. She'd come here. Sure, I'd invited her here, but she'd come on her own free will.

Now she was going to take me until I forgot about Kitt and that filthy fucker's hands on her.

But as I fucked Marlene, or was it Judy, I made sure to watch the screen as Kitt slept.

As long as she was in my line of sight, it would be okay.

CHAPTER 21

I take super hot showers because I like to practice burning in hell.
-Kitt to Ridley

Kitt

The next day I waved goodbye to my brother, who now sported a fucking tattoo exactly like Connor.

"Don't bend over for anything!" I called to Ridley as he started to walk down the drive to a truck that held some man behind the wheel that I'd seen before, but couldn't quite place.

Ridley stopped and turned, coming back to me to stop directly in front of my face.

"I told Freya if she wanted to come see you, or if she got lonely, that you'd be here. Watch out for her if she tries to make that connection, okay?" he asked.

I rearranged Emily in my arms, gently moving her so she was settled on my shoulder before holding out one arm to my brother.

Ridley promptly pulled me into his arms, letting his scratchy beard—a beard that still looked incredibly weird on him since he'd just started growing it out— play along my cheek.

I laughed and pushed him away, hating the itch that soon followed that move.

"I gave some guy your number at Wal-Mart today," I winked. "Will you be able to answer him?"

Ridley's face broke into a grin. "Yes, and it'll give me something to do."

I laughed, which woke Emily up.

Emily's head picked up from my shoulder, and she immediately turned to survey her surroundings.

Upon seeing her uncle, she reached for him.

Ridley promptly took her from my arms, gave her a small cuddle and a kiss, then handed her back to me.

Just as I had her settled back in my arms, Apple came out, looking like a badass.

His jeans were holey, and they looked like they were way past the point where they needed to be thrown away.

He had a black t-shirt stretched tightly over his chest, and his cut directly over that, denoting him a patched in member of The Uncertain Saints MC.

'CORE' was emblazoned in red over the breast pocket, and I might, or might not have, salivated slightly.

Luckily, I was holding Emily who was drooling like crazy due to the three teeth that were coming in at once, so I could easily play off the drool as hers if anyone called me on it.

"Damn," I muttered under my breath, my eyes assessing my man and his goods.

His hair was buzzed, and I found that I liked that.

A lot.

I'd seen him cut it last night while lying in bed, but with the early morning sunlight out over our heads, it really showed off his beautiful features.

His jaw was strong, his eyes hard and calculating.

The moment he saw me, though, they practically melted.

"You ready to lose your balls?" Ridley teased.

Apple's eyes looked from me to my brother, and his eyes shone.

"You ready to be sodomized?" He countered.

Ridley's grin grew, and Apple walked to him and offered his hand.

"You'll take care of her, won't you?" He demanded of Apple.

Apple nodded, and Ridley nodded back.

It must've been some guy code or something, because after whatever had just passed between the two was finished, they parted and Ridley walked away.

I waved at him as he got into the truck and buckled in, my heart in my throat.

"He'll be okay, baby," Apple said softly against my neck, pulling me in just long enough to place a long kiss on my collarbone before he walked to his bike.

"What are you doing?" I asked him.

"Riding to the doctor's office," he answered back almost immediately.

I blinked, surprised.

"You're what?" I asked. "You can't do that."

"Sure as fuck can if I want to," he muttered.

"What about us?" I asked. "How are we going to get there?"

"You're not," he said, starting his bike up and riding away before I could toss in another argument.

I snorted and walked to Ridley's new truck, buckling Emily into her car seat before walking around the front of the truck and getting inside.

I waited for about two minutes before Apple came back, parked next to the truck and got out, an annoyed look on his face.

He got into the truck without a word, slammed the door shut and started the truck up before backing sedately out of the driveway.

"You're just lucky I like this truck," he muttered darkly.

I snorted, turning my eyes to look out the window, noticing a car almost immediately parked about a hundred yards up from our house.

"Do you think they're broken down?" I asked, noticing the man in the front seat.

His eyes stayed locked on mine as we passed, and a shiver tore through me at the anger in the man's eyes.

The woman's eyes looked at me pleadingly, and my head notched slightly to the side when I saw the resemblance between her and me.

"Doubt it," he said. "I saw them pulling into the street when I turned out of it, and it was idling as I passed it by on the way back in.

I turned my head to study him.

"Are you sure you want to do this?" I asked him again.

He turned and his gaze connected with mine, smiles breaking out on both of our faces when a loud gurgle-scream pierced the silence between us from the backseat.

"I'm sure," he answered, finality ringing clear in his tone. "Never thought I'd get the one kid, and I don't want to go through that again with you."

I nodded in understanding.

"Just as long as you're sure," I reached for his hand.

He gave it willingly, and we held hands all the way to the doctor's office that would be performing Apple's vasectomy.

He held it all the way up until we shut the truck off, even backing up singlehandedly into the parking spot furthest from the door.

"Is there a reason we have to walk all the way across the parking lot when there were about ten parking spots closer?" I asked him.

He winked at me and got out, opening Emily's door and pulling her out, car seat and all.

I got the bag that was behind my seat, and we walked hand in hand to the office.

I never really put much thought into how sexy Apple actually was, but as we walked through the hospital corridor to the office where his procedure would be performed, he got not one, not two, but at least fifteen head turns from women of varying ages.

"You turned the head of every woman you passed since we got in here," I informed him as we got into the elevator.

"Likely, it was the patch," he pointed to his cut.

I snorted.

"That's it," I rolled my eyes.

He tossed me a sideways look, and I giggled.

"More than likely, it was those pants that you can almost see through," I told him.

He tossed me a look that clearly said he disagreed.

"They told me to wear something loose," he said. "I put these on because I have nothing but knit shorts, and those don't look good with my cut."

I rolled my eyes again.

The man was vain as hell about that cut.

He never went anywhere without it, and honestly, it didn't bother me much. It was just annoying. If I wanted to run to Sonic for an ice cream cone, he had to get completely dressed to do it, instead of wearing his shorts and a t-shirt like any other normal man in America.

No matter, he was proud as hell of that cut, and so was I. It was a symbol of Apple's growth. His step forward that changed both of our lives without his even meaning it to.

So yeah, I was proud as hell of that cut, too.

"Fuck," Apple muttered when the elevator doors slid open.

I tossed him a look, one that I hoped conveyed all my love and pride that I had for him and what he was doing.

We arrived at the glass doors that led to the receptionist, and I smiled wide when I saw a girl that used to be in my paralegal classes before I'd dropped out.

"Now," she said excitedly. "I've been waiting for months to meet the kiddo that led you out of that hell hole!"

I laughed and gestured for Apple to turn the car seat around for Katrina to see.

"Ohhhh," she whispered, leaning clear out the window. Looking up at Apple, she grinned. "She's the spitting image of you!"

I rolled my eyes.

Like I hadn't heard that before.

"There is no questioning whose kid she was at birth, that's for sure," I agreed with her.

Emily, at four days old, looked like her father, no doubt. But at a half a year old, the girl was his spitting image. Blue eyes with the ring of green around them.

Blonde curls, so pale, that they looked more white than blonde. The curls were so tight to her head that she resembled Shirley Temple.

Her smile was all him, too.

Katrina gushed over Emily, who, of course, took the attention with glee. She loved when people paid attention to her, something that wasn't like Apple or me.

"Okay," she said smiling. "Here's the paperwork. Do you have your insurance and ID?"

I handed Katrina my insurance card while Apple tried to stuff his large fingers into the leather pocket of his wallet to extract his license.

While he was fighting it, I smiled and turned to Katrina.

"How's school going?" I asked her.

She winced.

"Going as well as could be expected, I guess," she sighed. "I'm done in three more weeks, and I can't freakin' wait. I don't even know why I went into this in the first place. It's so depressing."

I knew what she was talking about. That was the very same thing I struggled with each and every time I went into school.

"I know what you mean," I sympathized. "But you're almost finished."

She sighed.

"When are you coming back?" She sounded so hopeful.

I shook my head in the negative. "I'm not."

Her eyes widened. "But you were so close to finishing!"

I shrugged and Apple placed a kiss on my forehead while he dropped his license onto the counter in front of Katrina.

"Going to fill this out, baby," he left, taking Emily with him.

I watched him take a seat as far away from the reception desk as he could, his back to the wall, and smiled before turning back to the front.

"I didn't like it," I explained. "And I don't think I could leave Emily right now. I'm enjoying this mommy thing."

Katrina was nodding with me.

"I can see that," she said. "Rob wants to try for some babies soon, too. I'm nervous."

I snickered.

Rob and her had been together for ten years. He was a mechanic at one of the shops in town, and he loved Katrina like crazy.

And it showed.

"Well, are you?" I asked.

We spoke in detail about her fears of having children since she was just starting out her career. So long, in fact, that Apple's name was called from the door leading back to the procedure rooms.

Apple stood, Emily in one arm, and his paperwork in the other and walked toward me.

"Love you, baby," he handed Emily over.

I took her and reached up to offer my lips to him, which he took.

"Be good for your mama," Apple instructed Emily.

Emily promptly barfed all over herself and me.

"Shit," I said, stepping to the side.

Apple laughed his ass off all the way to the door and to the woman that was still holding it open for him.

“Should I say ‘break a leg’?” I called to him.

He tossed me a glare over his shoulder.

I smiled and waved, blowing him a kiss.

He turned without answering the question, nor catching my kiss, and I snickered.

The woman closed the door, and I turned back to Katrina.

“Still want kids?” I teased.

Her eyes were wide.

“Did you just tell him to break a leg as he was going back to get a vasectomy?” she whispered.

I burst out laughing.

“Yeah, I did.”

She shook her head, and I laughed all the way back to the chair where Apple had left the car seat.

Placing Emily in it, I moved to the diaper bag.

But after searching it for clothes that I had put in the top of the bag just before leaving, I realized that they were gone and I didn’t have anything to change her into.

“Little girl,” I said to my daughter. “You need an award for inopportune puking.”

She gurgled, making me sigh.

She was cute; I’d give her that.

Groaning, I stood, taking her with me, picking up the keys that I kept in my diaper bag and headed to the door.

"I'll hold onto her for you," Katrina called to me as I reached the door.

I turned and handed her off.

"Thanks," I grimaced. "I think the clothes fell onto the floorboard of the truck."

She waved me off, and I hurried down the hall to the elevators.

I'd just stepped inside when a man stepped in with me.

I smiled at him out of habit, crowding myself into the very corner to allow him room.

He didn't turn around like most passengers did when they enter an elevator, though.

No, he got into the corner directly across from mine and stared.

I stared at the lights as they went from the third floor to the first floor and then ground level.

When the doors opened, I breathed out a sigh of relief and hurried out, thankful to get away from him and the uncomfortable way he made me feel.

What the hell had been up with him? And who didn't turn around and face the doors when they were in elevators.

Creeps, that's who.

Looking over my shoulder as I walked out through the main doors, I was thankful not to see him anymore.

Which was why I went to the truck instead of asking one of the security guys to walk with me like I probably should have. Especially when my gut churned with nerves, and my head was screaming at me to ask for an escort.

Thinking I would be just fine, I started weaving through the parking spots until I finally reached the truck.

Why Apple had to park so freakin' far away was beyond me, but I was winded with how fast I'd walked in order to hurry.

I'd just opened the backdoor to the truck when I felt someone creep up close to my side, likely wanting into their car.

"Sorry," I said when I sensed someone close. "These parking spaces sure are tiny, aren't they?"

Whoever it was didn't reply, so I looked up and immediately felt ice drift through my veins.

"Get in the truck," he demanded, pointing at the backseat.

I swallowed at the sight of the man in the elevator.

"I can't," I denied.

"You can," he informed me, lifting his jacket enough that I could see the gun he had hidden there. "Or I'll make you. Your choice."

I looked from him to the gun again, and then said, "You'll have to make me."

CHAPTER 22

Wicked chickens lay deviled eggs.
-Coffee Cup

Apple

A knock sounded on the door that was the only thing shielding my balls from the rest of the office, and I looked over at the doctor that had this fucking burning tool so close to my cock.

"You gonna get that?" I asked him.

"Yeah," he answered, leaning forward slightly. "As soon as I finish this one part."

The nurse that was helping looked over at me sympathetically.

"Dr. Norris hates interruptions," she smiled sympathetically. "He's on a schedule, and when people interrupt him, he has to get off that schedule."

"Schedules are made for a reason, Bridget. You should try to follow one sometime and you wouldn't be late to the office and interrupt my schedule every morning," he countered without looking at either of us.

I snorted and brought Bridget's eyes back to me.

"What Dr. Norris fails to mention is that I bring him coffee every morning, which is why I'm late to begin with," she informed me.

"What my wife fails to mention is that she could ride to work with me, if she would only be ready on time," he said. "But she's constantly late, and I leave her behind most mornings."

I would've replied, but the door opened without permission, bringing my attention away from Dr. Norris and Bridget, and to the lady that was, for some reason, holding my baby.

"Done! Bridget, please remove the sterile field, and we'll get him up and moving," Dr. Norris said. "Katrina, you better have a good reason for barging into this procedure room."

I didn't wait for Bridget to clear the field, I ripped the dressing off that was covering everything but my balls, and stood.

Katrina's eyes went wide at my cock hanging free, but something in the way she'd looked at me the moment she walked through the door had my heart nearly beating out of my chest.

"Where's Kitt?" I barked, walking to the chair that held my pants and yanked them on.

I ignored the fact that my balls screamed at me for that sudden movement.

"You need to sit down and wait until the glue at least dries," Dr. Norris scolded me. "Katrina, spit out whatever you need to say and get out!"

"I haven't seen your wife. I called security when she didn't come back, and they said some woman was abducted from the parking lot. I'm not sure if the woman is Kitt, but my gut says it is."

My eyes took in Emily, and a sense of relief so great hit me so hard and fast that I staggered as I buttoned my pants.

With Emily not being with Kitt, she'd be able to fight harder. She wouldn't be so worried about Emily that she'd forget to take care of herself.

"You really need to sit down, Sir," Bridget urged. "You're going to be a little woozy for the first hour or so, until all the medications we gave you wear off."

I ignored her, took a seat, and shoved my feet into my boots.

Once they were laced, I sat back up, grabbed my cut off the chair where the rest of my belongings had been and walked to Katrina.

"You okay with my baby?" He asked.

Katrina nodded hurriedly. "I am," she promised.

I nodded, pressed a kiss to Emily's forehead as she watched me curiously, then hurried down to the parking lot, my balls pinching with each stride I took.

By the time I made it to the first floor, I'd managed to call not only Peek, Wolf, Griffin, Casten and Mig, but the Sheriff as well.

The first person I found, as I made my way down to the parking lot, was a cop I'd never met before.

"The woman," I snapped without preamble. "She is mine."

The cop's shrewd dark eyes studied me, took in my cut and scars, then nodded his head.

All the while, I was seconds away from shaking him to get him to speak faster. I needed answers.

"Go on over there," he pointed to the back of the lot. "I'm just crowd control. The person you need to speak with is Officer Lyons."

I nodded my head and jogged to the back of the lot where I'd parked, sweat from the pain I was going through popping out all over my arms and face.

"Yo," the city cop that was directly next to the police line stopped me. "You can't come over here. Give it a few minutes and we'll release the vehicles to be moved.'"

"I don't give a fuck about my vehicle right now. I want to know who took my woman," I said through gritted teeth. "I need to know what you know."

"She your wife? Black hair down to her backside? Black tee and jeans?" he asked.

I nodded, the confirmation that it was in fact Kitt who'd been taken burning a hole in my gut.

"Yeah," I croaked. "That's her. Not my wife. Fiancé."

Well, she wasn't really that since I hadn't officially given her a ring yet. But she was mine. She was my old lady. Something I hadn't officially asked her to be, either. But I was planning on it. I just hadn't found a way to do it, yet.

I'd been too scared of her answer to do so just yet.

But now I was kicking myself for not asking her. Now it might be too late.

The sound of pipes had my heartbeat slowing, and I looked to the side to see Griffin and Wolf swing off their bikes.

They had offices that were right on the edge of the city limits. It wasn't a surprise that they were the first to arrive.

Marshall was only about a fifteen-minute ride if you went the speed limit, and I highly doubt either of them went the speed limit.

I turned back to the cop in front of me, then my eyes went to the truck where I could see Kitt's set of keys laying on the ground partially under the truck.

"What do you know?" I asked him.

"Witnesses say they saw a white male around the age of thirty-five or forty approach the woman from behind and cover her mouth with something, and the woman collapsed. She only got two screams out before she went limp, but she caught the attention of two elderly women who saw her being dragged into an older model navy blue Chevy Blazer. The Blazer II, not the full size," the cop explained.

Something sparked in my memory, and I closed my eyes and tried to trace that line.

No one interrupted me, but I could hear Wolf and Griffin asking questions of the officer as I thought, and then my heart started to pound.

"There was a smaller sized Chevy Blazer on our street today as I was leaving," I said. "Had a woman and a man in the front seat. Fits your description of thirty-five or forty. Our house has cameras and we can confirm. Was the feed pulled from the lot?" I asked the cop.

Another officer sauntered up, this one not in uniform, but plain clothes.

"Feed doesn't cover this lot. It's technically an overflow lot that's not owned by the hospital, but the city. Which means we don't have anything to pull," the plain clothes cop said.

My teeth gritted, and I turned to Wolf.

"Ridley has cameras set up outside and in. They run twenty-four seven and are monitored by a company that's out of Kilgore. Ridley shut off everything inside the house, but the stuff outside was left on because he liked the idea of having some security while he was gone," I told him. "You got anybody that could check that for us?"

Wolf nodded and paced a few feet away so he could make the call, and I turned to Griffin.

"You think you can get your woman up here to come get Emily?" I asked.

Griffin nodded and pulled his phone out of his pocket, walking away as well.

I turned back to the plain clothes.

"You have a BOLO out on the vehicle," I asked.

A BOLO was a 'be on the lookout' alert for law enforcement notifying them to watch for a particular vehicle or person as the case may be. So every cop in the area would be looking for this Blazer and my woman now.

"What about…" I stopped and turned when he pointed at something over my left shoulder.

"We have a woman in the ER across the street they found on the road about five miles South of here. She's telling some wild things, but there's a blue Chevy Blazer involved in this one, too. She's wanting to talk to a man named Apple."

My back stiffened at the young cop's words.

"Why?"

The young cop turned to me and said, "You Apple?"

I nodded.

“She has information about your lady,” he answered.

Five minutes later, and a pain pill thanks to a nurse who could clearly see I was hurting, I walked out of the ER doors and found the men of my MC waiting on me. We had interrogated the woman who was with the man who kidnapped Kitt.

“Whatcha got?” Peek asked, his accent thicker than normal.

“Woman is fucked up,” I blew out a breath. “Said she was thrown out onto the road once the mother fucker Jake took Kitt.”

“Jake?” Peek asked.

“Motherfucker who monitors the feed at our house,” I growled.

“Jake Carothers,” Wolf walked up with a packet of papers in his hand.

He handed them out to all of us and then to the cop that was standing off the side, Detective Mick Barrow, I’d learned.

My eyes went to Jake Carothers picture on the page, and I wanted to rip his face off.

“This is the same man I saw this morning as we were leaving,” I confirmed. “Where does he live?”

Wolf passed that paper out, too, conveniently leaving out the cop this time.

The cop noticed, too.

“Give me,” Barrow ordered.

Wolf held up his empty hands.

"Let's go," I said, hurrying to the truck that thankfully someone had pulled around for me.

I got in and Peek got in next to me.

Barrow hopped his happy ass in the back, and I wanted to scream at him to get out, but I didn't have time.

"Lenore have my baby?" I confirmed before I left the lot.

"Yep," Peek nodded.

I left the parking lot, and hit seventy within thirty seconds.

"Tell me where to go."

CHAPTER 23

Rise and shine, mothercluckers.
-Coffee Cup

Apple

"Put that away," Barrow ordered when he saw me pull a gun out from under the seat.

"No," I ignored him.

"I'll arrest you," Barrow said, his eyes hard and unwavering.

I lifted my brow at him.

"I was a cop, and I am a game warden. I'm not stupid. But you're not going to convince me to go in there without a gun. It's just not going to happen. Now, move the fuck out of the way, or I'll move you," I said through clenched teeth.

My shoulder was grabbed from behind and I turned to the front of the house and saw the best thing I'd ever witnessed in my life.

I started running toward Kitt, who looked at me in horror.

"Stop!" She insisted.

I stopped.

"Why?" I asked roughly.

"Because you just had surgery on your balls!" She whisper yelled.

I blinked and a few of the men started to snicker behind me.

I would've turned to glare at them, but the sight in front of me was too beautiful to turn away from.

"You okay?" I asked her, still not moving.

She nodded her head.

"Where's Jake?" I wanted to know.

"In hell," she replied through clenched teeth.

My eyes widened.

"Did you kill him?" I asked hopefully.

She shook her head again.

"No, but I'm sure he probably wishes he were dead right now," she informed me vaguely.

"Are you hurt?"

"No," she shook her head.

"Do you need me to carry you?"

"No," she repeated.

With that, I took myself, and my gun, around Kitt and walked straight into the house, and immediately started laughing.

"You stupid fucker," I snickered as I walked slowly up to the man that'd been watching my woman and creeping her out over the last year. "You're going to die."

The man didn't say anything.

He couldn't.

Not with his dick in his mouth like it was.

And literally. There was a dick in his mouth.

And, as I looked down at the mangled mess of meat and flesh between his legs, then back up to Jake, I wanted to laugh at him

Lifting my booted foot, I placed it along his groin and pressed, causing Jake to finally scream.

His balls were still there, so likely he wasn't feeling all too good right then.

"What the fuck's in his mouth?" Griffin asked as he came up to my back.

"His dick," I answered.

"Did you do that?" Wolf sounded pained.

I shook my head.

"Who did?" Barrow asked, looking dispassionately down at the man's balls that I had pinned to the floor.

"My guess is that my woman did it," I answered, twisting my foot.

All of the men that were at my back cringed when we heard something inside his balls pop.

"I think that's enough," Barrow sighed. "Back away please."

I did, but only after the second testicle popped, too.

***

I had Emily in one arm, and Kitt in the other, as we stood outside the house.

"We're not going to tell Ridley a damn thing," Kitt insisted. "Because he has enough to worry about right now without adding me to the mix."

"He's going to want to know," I tried to be the voice of reason, but Kitt wasn't having it.

"Is he your brother?" She snapped.

I held onto my smile.

"Yes," I said, and it was true.

He may not be my flesh and blood brother like he was to her, but he was my brother. My MC brother, and in some cases, that was tighter than blood would ever be.

Certainly not in this case.

Ridley and Kitt were like two peas in a pod.

Ridley and me, not so much. But we tolerated each other, and I wouldn't hesitate to come to his aid or even go and have a beer with him.

She sighed in defeat.

"I don't want to tell him, because I want him to focus on what he's doing in there. I don't want his head to be anywhere but where it's supposed to be," she whispered. "Please?"

That 'please' paired with those big green eyes of hers, and I was a fucking goner.

"Okay," I said. "But the moment he steps foot outside, I'm telling him. He's not going to hear about it from anyone but me."

"What about the rest of you?" Kitt asked, looking around at the rest of The Uncertain Saints.

Not a single one of them was trying to hide the fact that they were paying attention to our conversation.

But wasn't that what brothers did? Butt into your business?

"Up to you, Core," Griffin said. "You tell us what you want to do, and we'll do it…maybe."

Kitt growled, and it was so cute that I pulled her into my arms again and kissed her forehead.

"Chill, baby," I urged. "He's joking."

"Am I?" Griffin challenged, a small smirk kicking up the corner of his lips.

I looked up to the sky where we were still waiting outside the stupid fucker's house, and smiled for the first time in over an hour.

"By the way," Griffin asked, changing the subject. "How are your balls?"

"Can't even feel 'em," I said honestly. "That pill the chick at the hospital gave me is making me feel no pain."

"What chick?" Kitt asked, stiffening in my arms.

"Her name was Hannah. I met her before in one of our many trips to the ER." I said. "She took pity on me when she saw me grimacing when we were questioning the stand in that Jake kicked out of the car."

This time Wolf was the one who stiffened.

"Hannah?" Wolf asked, "What'd she look like?"

"Blonde. Big tits. Long hair down to her ass. The bluest eyes I've ever seen," I recalled.

Kitt pinched me on my side.

"You're not supposed to say that you noticed her tits when your woman's in your arms," she hissed.

I looked down into her face, took in her angry eyes, and said innocently. "My woman's not in my arms. My old lady is."

She blinked.

"I'm not old," she said testily.

I grinned.

"Oh, darlin'. You most certainly are. Trust me," I said, pulling her to the truck and away from the rest of the group before this got too heated.

She took Emily from my arms and put her into her car seat, and I watched in fascination as Wolf ran past me, hopped on his bike and was out in a spit of gravel and dust.

"What was that about?" I demanded of Griffin who passed me to get to his bike.

His woman went to her car that was next to Griffin's bike, but stopped and turned to say, "That was Wolf going to get *his* Old Lady."

Then a commotion came from the house as a screaming Jake was finally pulled from the house.

Tears and snot mingled on his face as he sobbed, and I couldn't help the full out shit eating grin that transformed my face.

"Hope you have fun in jail!" I called to him.

His eyes turned to me, and I couldn't help the laugh that escaped my lips at seeing the blood still around his mouth. Remembering how it got there would forever be ingrained in my memory, and I chose to remember her walking out with a grin on her face rather than having to be in that position in the first place.

Fucking A.

"Apple?" Kitt called from inside the cab of the truck.

I turned and got in.

"What?" I asked.

"Does being your old lady come with a ring?" She batted her eyes sweetly.

I smiled at her.

"Fuck yeah it does," I said. "I have some chicken rings at my place we can cook up for dinner."

She slapped my arm in affront.

"That's not what I meant, and you damn well know it."

I fluttered my eyelashes at her, and she rolled her eyes.

"You're incorrigible."

"I'm fucking happy."

"You may be fucking happy, but you're still incorrigible."

I shrugged.

"No, baby. I'm happy," I said. "I haven't been that in a very, very long time."

Her eyes went soft, and I started the truck up, turning back to the road and heading in the opposite direction of home.

"Where are you going?" She asked softly.

"To *Sams* to get some more chicken rings for my old lady," I said.

We didn't go to *Sams*.

We went to *Jared's*.

Where Kitt proceeded to tell everyone and their brother in a seemingly endless flurry of text messages.

Thirty minutes later when she walked in to my pop's place and shoved the ring in his face, I couldn't find it in me to care that she kept repeating the same sentence over and over again.

"He went to Jared's!" She crowed. "Yee haw!"

My pop smiled at her indulgently.

"That's good, sweet girl," my dad slurred slightly. "Now, maybe, he can stop fucking around and get some of that wood cut up."

Kitt got the baby out of her car seat and handed her over to my father, and I turned to survey the woodpile my dad had just gestured to.

"You did good, boy," my dad said to my back.

I turned back to look at my dad who was now holding Emily, then looked at Kitt who was on her phone with one of the old ladies, and I walked to the wood and started cutting it up.

The life I lead may not be perfect, but it was mine. And that was perfect to me.

EPILOGUE

Sorry I'm late. I didn't set my alarm. I didn't set my alarm because I didn't want to come.
-Kitt's secret thoughts

Kitt

Two months later

"I need you to come inside," I whispered into the telephone.

"Why are you whispering?" Apple asked, sounding somewhat alarmed.

"Because it'll hear me," I whispered back.

"What'll hear you?" Apple asked, fully alarmed at this juncture.

As he should be.

"There's a bug. A cockroach. In the middle of the kitchen floor. He's talking to his friend, Mrs. Cockroach," I continued whispering.

"Jesus Christ," he said. "Just step on it."

"No. Come inside or I'll scream," I ordered.

He sighed, and hung up, and I hoped that meant he was coming.

And twenty seconds later when the door opened, I was happy to know he'd complied.

But the man who stepped into the kitchen was most assuredly *not* Apple.

"Step on them!" I ordered, pointing to the bugs.

He did, stepping on them with a loud crunch that threatened to cause me to lose my lunch.

"Where is he?" Ridley snapped.

My eyes widened at the anger in his voice.

Apple stepped in through the backdoor, and I turned to see Ridley launch himself at him.

"You can't just not tell me that!" Ridley pushed Apple.

I sighed and started forward, knowing exactly where this was going.

"No, he can't. But I can," I said, pushing my brother back.

He looked fucking crazy rough, and I was actually a little intimidated by the fact that he'd bulked up so much while in prison.

He didn't look like the old Ridley, but a new, harder Ridley.

One that was hell bent on vengeance, and I wasn't sure I liked it.

But he was my brother, and I knew all his ire wasn't due to the fact that he was mad at anyone, but rather it was concern for me.

"Ridley!" I cried out loudly. "Would you listen to me for a freakin' minute?"

He turned his glare on me, and I smiled at him before running toward him.

He'd walked into the house today without even telling me he was coming and then proceeded to start yelling.

How he'd known before we'd told him about it, I didn't know. But there was no use figuring it out now. What was done was done, and my brother was now home.

He caught me and wrapped both of his large arms around my shoulders, and I buried my face into his neck.

"I missed you, big brother," I whispered.

"Missed you, too," he said gruffly. "Proud of you. And sorry. Really fucking sorry."

I squeezed him tighter, and then tilted my head back to study his face.

"What's going on with you?" I asked. "You look rough."

"Lots of shit that I do not want to talk about right now," he said. "I want to drink a beer and watch you get married."

I smiled at him.

"How are you going to pull that off?" I asked him. "We're already married."

His eyes narrowed.

"Don't think we're not going to talk about that, either," he growled. "Vegas? Really?"

I smiled at him and pulled away, walking to the kitchen where Emily was busy making a mess of her applesauce.

"Watch this," I called to Ridley. "You're going to be so surprised!"

Emily automatically reached for me the instant I got to her, and I pulled the tray back on the highchair then hooked my hands under her armpits.

Immediately, I set her down on the floor, and she sat there staring at her uncle who came in looking a lot scruffier than when he'd left.

"Call her," I said to him.

I moved to the kitchen counter and leaned my behind against it directly next to Apple who immediately hooked an arm around my neck and pulled me in close.

"Emily," Ridley called, dropping down onto his haunches.

Emily's head whipped around from watching Apple and me to her uncle, and her mouth opened wide into a single tooth baby grin.

"Oh, man," he said. "You got your first tooth while I was gone."

Drool started to leak out of her mouth, and she leaned forward until she was on her belly.

Then she immediately started to army crawl to Ridley, who thought it was the cutest thing in the world. Mostly because he'd said so.

"Oh Jesus," he groaned when she started making her way to him. "Fucking cutest thing in the world."

I snorted and laughed when he dropped to his ass and then crossed his legs.

Leaning forward, he scooped her up the instant she was within reach and then covered her with kisses.

His shirt became soaked with applesauce, but he didn't seem to care.

Emily had changed a lot in the last two months. She'd gotten her first tooth a couple of weeks prior.

She'd also gotten her first major boo-boo that had required a trip to the ER.

An ER visit where she was treated for a laceration over her right eye.

And that had been my fault.

I'd left her on the couch like I'd done so many times before, but instead of staying there, she'd fallen off, in her search for me, and had cut her head open on the coffee table.

I'd been promised by not just the ER docs, but also by the other ladies in the club that had children that accidents happened. Frequently.

She'd also finally started to sleep through the night and eat solid foods.

I'd stopped breast-feeding, and we'd switched over to only formula in hopes that she would stop throwing up so much.

Which she did.

And she, as did my life in general, became a whole lot sweeter with less vomit.

Apple had also done a lot of changing.

He'd continued his trips to his psychologist to help him with the guilt and pain he suffered, even now.

And he got a lot better. I could definitely see a change in him, that was for sure.

He hadn't told them his real reasons for being there, only touched on the fact that his friend had died, but he'd told them all that he could, and they'd been able to help him come to terms with a few things.

He'd also stopped working so much overtime as a game warden when he could. When hunting season rolled around two weeks ago, I'd lost him again. And I was sure that would happen every hunting season. But a plus was that his father had completely closed his wood cutting business.

Now Apple only cut wood for fun in his spare time.

And I was one happy person.

My seizures, although still present, were back to my normal. Which meant every once in a while I would space out for about thirty seconds, and then I would snap back.

I hadn't had one more bad seizure since I'd been placed on the lowest dose of anti-seizure medication available.

And I was fucking ecstatic about that.

Life was good.

"So tell me what happened with the douche canoe that kidnapped you," Ridley ordered.

I looked up at Apple, then to Emily.

"I'm going to go give Emily a bath while you boys talk," I said softly, picking Emily from Ridley's arms and hurrying away. "And get ready to go to lunch! I'm hungry!"

I didn't wait for a reply.

It wasn't that I was embarrassed by what I did to Jake.

In fact, I was okay with it. Happy, in fact.

That day two months ago had been terrible.

I wasn't sure if I was going to live or die and that had a way about bringing out the worst in a person.

What I'd experienced with Jake was not nice. It was not pretty, and to be honest, it haunted my nightmares.

Every night my dream would be the same.

I'd wake up after passing out from him covering my mouth to being in a chair. A chair that I was not tied down to or anything.

I looked around at the room, taking in the knives on the kitchen counter, as well as the baseball bat that was leaning against the wall in the corner behind the door.

Once I was sure my legs would hold me, I stood up and walked carefully to the bat.

A knife was nice and all, but that would put me too close to the person that'd taken me, and I needed distance.

Once the solid weight was in my hand, I looked around at the room I was in.

The house I was in was only a single open room with large beams acting as support. It looked like it'd recently been remodeled to look like this, because the drywall was still exposed over most of the walls and there were tools all over the place.

My next step was to look outside and, once there, I saw the same man that I'd seen in the elevator earlier.

"What the hell is going on?" I whispered, running across the room to the closed door.

I waited there, watching him do something outside on the porch, for what felt like hours but was likely only minutes.

Then he turned. There was something that looked like plastic bags and tape in his hand, as he reached for the doorknob.

The moment he opened the door and stepped inside, I'd come up at his back and slammed the bat upside his head.

He dropped like a stone.

When he'd come to, he'd been the one taped to the chair.

I'd been the one asking questions, and what I'd heard hadn't been nice.

In fact, it's downright sickening.

Hearing what he'd done to the woman before, one that looked so much like me that it could've been me, had flipped my switch and left me feeling cold.

The icing on the cake had been him coming at me with said dick in his hand, ready to do the same damn thing to me.

Which was the reason I did what I did next.

Everyone knows the story from there.

Apple had been so proud of me that it was hard to feel bad about it. I'd been appalled at my actions but something had come over me at hearing that man's promise that he would do the same thing to me. And the next lady he felt like doing it to.

And I couldn't let that happen. So I'd done what I had to do, and had nightmares about it as a consequence.

During each nightmare, though, Apple would be there to chase the bad away.

He'd wake me up with a soft kiss to my lips, and then hold me while the remnants of the dream drifted away into nothing.

He hadn't been able to convince me to speak with anyone, either.

Why? Because why would I when I had my own personal dream catcher that chased away the bad dreams for me? Why would I need to speak to someone that couldn't do for me what Apple could?

"Oh, baby," I said when I saw the mess Emily had made of herself. "You're a big ol' mess."

She chattered away at me while I got her changed into her clothes for the day.

Tonight would be a welcome home party for Ridley, and I was fairly sure we would be spending the night at the clubhouse in celebration. Likely a good bit of us would be drunk and too smashed to drive home, so I made sure to grab some extra clothes and diapers to take with us.

Once Emily was dressed, I took her to my room and let her play on the floor while I folded laundry and genuinely ignored the living room where I knew Ridley and Apple were talking.

I'd gone through three whole loads of laundry before I felt Apple's presence at my back.

"You okay?" he asked, coming up behind me and wrapping both arms around my belly.

I nodded and leaned my head against his chest.

"I'm fine," I said. "Embarrassed."

He rubbed his beard along my neck and said the words I expected to hear.

The same ones that I heard every single time that memory assaulted me.

"You know how hot it makes me thinking about how you handled yourself," he rumbled softly. "Knowing you went all Lorena Bobbitt on the stupid fucker is so goddamned hot, all I want to do is fuck you."

I laughed softly. The Lorena Bobbitt bit was new, but the 'making him hot' wasn't.

He was proud of what I'd done, and I was proud to make him proud.

It was a win-win situation.

"Where's my brother?" I whispered, letting my hands come up to tangle in his hair.

"Took Emily to him. He's gonna watch her for a minute or fifteen," he answered.

I snorted.

"Okay, my brother can stay in my house if there are conveniences like this," I whispered to him, turning around in his arms.

I pressed a kiss to his lips and wrapped my arms around his neck.

He pulled my hips forward until the length of me was pressed to the length of him.

“You’re happy to see me,” I sighed, grinding my hips into his cock.

He growled.

“I’m always happy to see you.” And I was.

ABOUT THE AUTHOR

Lani Lynn Vale is married to the love of her life that she met in high school. She fell in love with him because he was wearing baseball pants. Ten years later they have three perfectly crazy children and a cat named Demon who likes to wake her up at ungodly times in the night. They live in the greatest state in the world, Texas. She writes contemporary and romantic suspense, and has a love for all things romance. You can find Lani in front of her computer writing away in her fictional characters' world...that is until her husband and kids demand sustenance in the form of food and drink.

CPSIA information can be obtained
at www.ICGtesting.com
Printed in the USA
LVHW051438271218
601919LV00015B/716

9 781537 157696